Zippy

M-Gang Chronicles: Book One

———————————

Robert Linus Koehl

Zippy (M-Gang Chronicles: Book One)

Copyright © 2012 Robert Linus Koehl

Parts of this book are based on true events, however, these segments have been fictionalized and all persons appearing in this work are fictitious. Any resemblance to real people, living or dead, is entirely coincidental. Any actions by celebrities or politicians described herein were strictly fictional.

The actions of government agencies, including Mossad, Shin-Bet, the Plano Police Department, and Plano Independent School District, are entirely fictionalized. Any similarities to actual actions taken by any of these agencies or their employees is strictly coincidental.

Edited by Judy Koehl and Robert Linus Koehl.

Original Edition Edited by Roslyn Gonzalez, Cindy Goodman, and Lysette Koehl. Published by Robert Koehl – Dallas TX, USA

ISBN: 0985783338
ISBN 13: 978-0985783334 (Robert\Koehl

First Edition ISBN: 0985783303
First Edition ISBN 13: 978-0985783303 (Robert\Koehl
UNITED STATES)
LCCN: 2012911821

PREFACE

I came up with the idea while walking through downtown Fort Worth on a lovely spring morning in 2009. I first told this story to my girlfriend Roslyn while we were sitting in at the Superpages Center (formerly Starplex Ampetheatre) in Dallas. We were waiting for a Depeche Mode concert to begin, and she asked me to tell her a story. She'd frequently make this request of me and my mind would always blank when she'd say it . . . but not that day. I told her about Mark and Zippy's adventures. Of course, the story was much longer than the one you're about to read . . . I guess that's my way of saying there will hopefully be a sequel . . . hopefully.

Major thanks to Roslyn, Cindy, my parents, Lysette, Eric, Carolyn, Steve, Alyson, Fred, Bianca, my grandparents, cousins, aunts, uncles and other "inner sanctum" folks. Also props to Jack and all the other folks who taught me Krav Maga . . and to Deb, who had the foresight to start a Children's Krav Maga program in the US. I assure all readers that they're not recruiting assassins - just teaching kids how to handle scary situations, should they ever arise.

And finally to the Baruch HaShem Synagogue in Dallas. You guys cued me in to SO MANY THINGS that I'd been missing my entire life.

TABLE OF CONTENTS

TABLE OF CONTENTS (CONT'D)

PROLOGUE – FOUR YEARS AGO

Thursday, May 8, 1986

The wind blew relentlessly. Not that this was any source of relief or comfort. In the mid-afternoons of May in the suburbs of Dallas, the wind was just one more reason why it was hot. The ground was hot, the air was hot, and the wind was like mother nature's blow-dryer.

School had been out for half an hour and most of the kids had run home, been picked up by the long string of mommy cars out front, or were hitting the playgrounds behind the building. But there was one group of 8-year old boys by the creek behind the playground. Four of them were surrounding the smallest of the bunch. He wasn't their friend. He had no desire to be anywhere near there. But the teachers were all looking elsewhere. There was nobody to stop what was happening.

The four larger boys were having a great time watching the little one break down and cry as they shoved him around. The more frightened he became, the harder they'd shove him. This continued until one of the bullies shoved him to the ground. As he fell, one of his hands landed in a fire ant mound. He screamed. All four of his tormenters laughed. He panicked, slamming his hand into the grass as quickly as he could. Hundreds of ants had swarmed upward the moment he fell, covering his arm with venomous stings. He scrambled to his feet and ran towards the creek, batting madly at his hand, trying to knock the ants off. But the ants were already getting into his shirt and stinging his chest.

As he threw himself into the rancid creek water, the giggling from the four boys behind him grew into an all-out chorus of laughter. He was slapping the ants off one by one, but they were still biting - nobody ever told him that fire ants cling to your body under water. They'll drown before giving up a chance to inject their poison. His hand was already swelling. It would probably reach more than twice its size within the hour.

The boys eventually turned and ran. They'd pressed their luck for long enough. Much better to let the teachers catch the little nerd flailing about in the creek than to be caught anywhere near the creek themselves. He'd probably even get in trouble with the teachers for being so near the creek.

As they fled, one the boys noticed the girl. She was leaning against a tree about a hundred feet away, taking advantage of the shade. She was around their age, but none of them recognized her. She didn't go to their school, and she was dressed funny. She had on some sort of formal dress, like what you'd expect a girl to wear to Sunday School - on a Thursday afternoon in May. And the dress was really messed up. It was covered in something that looked like mud. Her face was absolutely devoid of emotion, like some statue in a museum. And that statue was watching them.

The boys all stopped running. The largest of the four boys shouted at her, "Hey!! You didn't see any of this!! Got it? If anyone asks, the moron was playing by the creek, and he just fell in."

Her face didn't change.

The four boys started walking towards her, "I mean it. One word to a teacher and you'll get the same."

Her face still didn't change.

The largest boy stopped and looked around at his three friends, "I think this stupid girl wants to go for a swim herself." They all chuckled in agreement.

Her face changed, but she didn't look afraid. She was smirking. Her eyes looked hungry. She began whispering in a language that none of the boys had ever heard before. She started to walk towards them like she was about to pick a fight.

They had no idea what to make of her. Every last thing about this girl was wrong, and that babble she was whispering sounded creepier with every step she took. Somehow each of the boys felt a sudden burst of terror.

This girl was dangerous.

They scattered into four different directions, running for life and limb before any of them could find out just what was behind that scary smile.

Their victim's cries from the creek were now loud enough that a teacher came running. He would soon be rushed to the emergency room, as that many fire ant bites would cause most adults to go into shock, to say nothing of a small child.

But the girl turned and walked the other way, as though she'd just watched a bunch of kids playing normal playground games. Nothing particularly special had happened - just a bunch of kids doing what kids do. When she heard the ambulances approaching, an odd smile broke across her face. She continued walking. Once the school was long behind her, she began whistling a happy little tune.

And the wind kept blowing relentlessly.

CHAPTER ONE – LOST IN THE DARKNESS

Saturday, March 3, 1990

When I was seven, I really loved this movie called "Fright Night." It wasn't exactly Oscar worthy, but to a little kid in the mid-1980s, it was the ultimate horror film. Anyway, there was a character named "Evil Ed." He was an absolute nerd. He got picked on and pushed around by his classmates a LOT. They nicknamed him "Evil" because he looked funny and he was really into horror movies. So at one point, the bad guy (a vampire named Jerry Dandridge) had Ed cornered in an alleyway. Ed was so frightened that he was shaking and crying uncontrollably. He knew he was about to die.

Dandridge just stood there with this caring, empathetic look on his face. He promised that nobody would ever pick on Ed again. And like a loving big brother, he said "All you have to do is take my hand." Then he smirked, holding out this scary looking claw. "Here Edward, take my hand."

I think of that scene every time I think about the

weekend those seven kids showed up in the alleyway behind my house. I had my boom-box sitting out in the driveway, blaring The Cure's "Disintegration" album. I'd only had the tape for about a week or so, but I already knew the words to most of the songs.

Ordinarily if a kid my own age would come walking up the alleyway, I'd grab my boom-box, race into the garage, close the door, and then wait till the coast was clear.

But for some reason, I'd gotten careless that Saturday evening. I was playing a few rounds of basketball before dinner. I was mid-throw, the first verse of "Fascination Street" was playing, and I heard a girl's voice over my shoulder - "That's him!!!!"

My heart shot up into my throat. I spun around. The ball bounced off the backboard and went bouncing - bounce bounce bounce - off into the alleyway, only to be picked up by the most muscled-up boy I'd never seen. Seven kids were walking up towards me.

"That's him!!!" The girl was Sheri Azel. She was in my orchestra class. There was also Danny. I didn't know his last name. He was from my school, too. And there was Zippy.

Zippy had been my best friend last summer. We'd ridden our bikes all over the neighborhood. We'd hung out at each other's houses. There was even this hilarious incident when we rode our bikes over to an abandoned construction site. Zippy got off her bike and walked over to the lone blue porta-potty which stood like a landmark in the middle of this mess. She looked back at me with a devious smirk and said, "I always wanted to do this." Then she kicked the porta-potty. And MY GOD could she EVER kick hard!!! BAM - the whole thing tipped over. SPLASH!!!! Bright blue chemicals went running everywhere. And these little white lumps that had once been poop were sailing down the blue stream. It sounds gross, I know. But if you'd seen it, you'd laugh at the image in your head. I certainly do.

But those days were long over. If Zippy was hanging out with kids from my school, she probably wasn't going to be my friend any more. Nobody in their right mind would want to be. I didn't recognize the others. All total, there were four girls and three boys.

I was dead. I knew this routine. They would act all friendly, surround me, then it would scary, and then they would hurt me. It had happened several times a week.

"So this is Cohen?" said one of the boys.

"Yes," Zippy said with her typical playfulness, "this is Mark Cohen."

One of the other girls walked over to my boom box and turned it off. Usually, this would be a capital crime as far as I was concerned, but right now I was too scared to say anything about it. I just wanted to get out of this situation with my boom box and body intact . . . and maybe even my basketball. This girl looked like Zippy. They were both Middle-Eastern, but this girl had longer hair and . . . wow, eyelashes that were upside down. They literally curved downward, partially blocking her eyes. She said something to Zippy in a language I didn't recognize.

"English, Sivan. Mark doesn't speak Hebrew." Zippy was being a little too playful, and the boys were getting a little too close. "We've come to talk to you, Mark. I've been hearing things about you, and I want to know if they're true."

Damn. If she'd been listening to Sheri or any of the kids in my school, then they'd probably filled her head with the lies that have been going around about me. Those same lies caused all my friends to quit talking to me. They caused everyone to know my name, and they caused everyone to think it's okay to hurt me. Maybe it showed on my face, because Zippy seemed to just know. She turned her head slightly. "You've nothing to-"

"People have been talking a lot of trash about me,

Zipps. But it's all a bunch of crap. I don't know what Sheri told you, but-"

"Sheri say no bad about you." Zippy was an immigrant from the Middle East. She tried to make up for English being her second language by learning as many hard vocabulary words as possible, but she never seemed to get things like word order and sentence structure correct.

My mind was racing - desperately trying to figure out a way out of this situation. Sheri suddenly piped up, "Mark, I've seen the stuff that's been happening to you at school. I told Zippy about the rumors, but I don't think they're . . . true or anything. I just told her what I've . . . you know."

"He's scared." The upside-down eyelash girl actually DID speak English. I didn't know if she was taunting me, but she was right. I was scared out of my wits. I'd been through this a few times too many not to be.

"You're right, Sivan," Zippy was looking right at me, but she wasn't taunting. She looked like a doctor who was examining a wound. "He's scared. He thinks we here to hurt him."

Great diagnosis, doc.

"Amir, stick around. The rest of you, go back to my place. Let's show Mark just how much he has to be afraid of." They all shrugged. Upside-Down Eyelash Chick protested "Are you going to be coddling him if he joins? You're being weird with this one."

Zippy turned and hissed something in Hebrew to her - at least I assumed it was Hebrew. I couldn't pretend to know. But it must have been something harsh because cause all the others kids gasped.

It didn't affect Upside-Down Eyelash Chick at all. She just looked at me with a half-smile, like she wanted to call me a wimp. She shook her head with the slightest bit of disgust, then walked away. Sheri and Danny both had the same concerned look that Zippy did, but they both walked off too. So did all the others . . all but Zippy and one of the larger boys. He had a crew-cut hairdo and he was wearing a muscle shirt to show off how tough he was. He and Zippy both wore identical necklaces - a Jewish Star of David symbol with some weird writing superimposed over it.

"I know you were scared of us. I understand why, but you never to be afraid of me. I'm your friend, Mark."

"I know."

"No, you don't! Sheri tell to me what happen to you over the last month. I know you think 'friend' is just someone who turn into one of the bullies who beat you up when other kids want them to. I'm no this person."

"I know, Zipps." I was probably the only person on the planet who could get away with calling her that. I'd seen another boy call her "Zipps" once. It wasn't pretty. But she let me, and me alone, call her by this nickname.

She sighed and looked down at the ground in front of her. "No you don't, Mark. If you knew, then you no would have been scared. You WERE scared, so you thought we might hurt you. What you need to know is that whenever I am with you, you to never need be scared."

It didn't make much sense, but as I sat there looking at her, she seemed so sure of what she was saying. I didn't know what to say.

She took me by the hand and looked directly into my eyes. "Why don't you tell me what happening to you. What make you so afraid?"

It took me a few seconds to decide. I hadn't even told my mom and dad some of this stuff. I didn't want to talk to Zippy about it either.

Zippy represented a happier time before things started really going wrong in my life. We'd been best friends last summer but I hadn't really seen her much since then. And I wanted to keep the dark parts of my life separate from the clean parts . . . from her. But she wasn't going to let me do that.

"Come on Mark." Her voice was getting even softer.

"Tell to me what happen."

What did I have to lose? What's the worst she'd do? Laugh at me? Have this muscle-guy beat the crap out of me? I might hear about this from laughing voices at school on Monday, but right now I had the chance to simply let it out.

"It started about a month ago. It was on a Tuesday. I was out of school all day cause I was getting my braces put on. While I was out, a couple of kids started a rumor about me."

"This is the rumor about the bathrooms." Yep, Zippy had heard alright.

"Yeah, but they're not true."

"I never say they were." She was 13 − nearly a year older than me − but her face and mannerisms were more like an adult.

I continued, "Well, it's more fun to think they're true. It's fun for people to think that there's a kid who does things with other boys in the bathrooms for money. People say they believe the rumors because 'they're true,' but they're not. They believe them cause they want to."

"Mark, I've heard this story before. Someone get everyone else to hate you, so everyone else hurt you for them. We Jews call it 'blood libel.' It happened to our people for many centuries. What next?"

I paused for a moment. What was she talking about? Whatever it was, I knew what was next all too well. I'd gone over it in my head dozens of times.

"I went to school that Wednesday, and they were in the library - the kids who started the rumors: Dusty and Sam. They started going person to person saying 'hey, did you hear about Mark Cohen' and then they started telling this story. Dusty claimed Sam caught me. Sam claimed Dusty caught me."

"How you respond?"

"I didn't. I thought 'screw em, if these guys have

nothing better to do than make up stuff like a bunch of giggling girls, then I've got no use for them.' It sounded good in my head anyway."

Oh no!! A huge lump started forming in my throat. I didn't want to start crying – not in front of Zippy. She'd never think of me as "cool" again.

I tried to keep it together and continue. "I was more worried about the throbbing in my mouth from these damned braces. I'd just got them put on the day before. My gums were so bruised . . . I didn't know how eager everyone at school was to believe gross things about me. The rumor spread around the school. By the end of the week, all 900 kids thought I was gay."

"Not all 900." She looked ever so serious as she said it. "Some kids were disgusted by what was happening to you and what people saying about you."

"You mean Sheri and Danny?"

She smiled a bit. "They have been taught to look at things with a certain . . . perspective."

"Well, it doesn't matter. Every day for the past month, I've gotten beat up - usually by a gang of three to six guys at a time." The lump was REALLY making its presence known and my voice was starting to crack. I wasn't going to be able to hold out long.

"What about the teachers?"

"They usually look the other way. One said it's not her job to be a cop. And last week I got caught running from a kid who was trying to hurt me, and I got a detention for running in the hall. They didn't care what I was trying to get away from. And then . . ."

Zippy's gaze went blank, like she was looking inside me.

I continued, ". . . then there's the whispers in the hall. *'Psst, there goes the faggot.' 'Hey, you got 3 dollars.' 'There goes the blowjob man, if he can't suck it nobody can.'* Sometimes people make slurping noises when I walk by. There were a few times when someone walked up and spit on me. I can't sit down at any table at lunch time cause kids will throw food at me. They like to throw hotdogs at me and say things like 'suck on this one for us, show us how to blow.' And . . . then there's the boy's locker room."

I felt the first tear go down my cheek. I was going to cry right here in front of Zippy and Muscle Guy. I'd only broken down and cried maybe once or twice since this whole nightmare began. That had only given the kids at school more material to laugh at me with. But Zippy wasn't laughing. Her face had gone from concerned to angry.

I kept going, "They like to gang up on me in the locker room. They're always trying to grab me. It always gets . . it's bad. There's nowhere to run and sometimes they don't JUST want to beat me up in there. Sometimes they . . ."

I was openly crying now. No sense hiding it. Muscle Guy looked like he wanted to give me a hug. Zippy looked like her blood was boiling. Muscle Guy spoke up "This ain't your fault, man. You know that, right?"

Zippy looked at him "Do you think that matters? When these things happen, fault or no fault, they still happen." She looked back at me. "Mark, what happened on Valentine's Day?"

How the hell did she know about that?

"The school had a letter exchange. You could write a Valentine to anyone and the school would deliver it to them. I got about 100 letters from different people claiming to be 'Dave,' this guy that I'd supposedly done all these things with. Every letter described these disgusting things that I'd supposedly done . . . or disgusting things that this guy wanted to do . . . I can't even get away from it at home. People call me on the phone and say all kinds of things and-"

I couldn't get the words out. My throat was just getting too tight for me to talk. I was openly sobbing. Zippy leaned forward and hugged me. "You're lost in the darkness. Let me help you escape from it."

She knew. Somehow, she knew exactly how I felt. This entire month had become a scar on my life. I'd go home every day and do my best to forget the previous 7 hours. I'd get to the weekend and try to pretend the whole week didn't happen.

I completely broke down. "You're right about my friends. Nobody wanted to know me. Nobody wanted to be seen talking to me. I wasn't very popular as it was. I only had a few friends. But as soon as the rumors started, they all just joined the crowds, making fun of me, throwing food at me at lunch time . . ."

"You've got friends now." Muscle Guy wasn't boasting. He didn't sound proud or anything when he said it. He didn't even smile. "I'm Amir." He reached out and shook my hand.

"Things start changing for you now." Zippy sounded so sure of herself.

"Thank you." I couldn't think of anything else to say.

"It will no be easy. We can no just make them stop, but we also must to change how you think. We need to make you . . a little more like us. Make you so you can make them stop. Make you so that you can keep it from ever starting again. Make you say 'never again.'"

"What do you mean?"

"Mark, listen to me." She paused for a few seconds to think about her words. "There are two types of people in this world. There are those who wake up in middle of night, find themselves in the darkness, try to adjust their eyes, and feel their way around the room, hoping they no run into something or stub their toe. Then there are those who just turn on the damned light. YOU try to adapt to the darkness around you. I want to make you turn on the light. You no understand this right now, but you will eventually."

She said something in Hebrew to Amir, then looked back at me.

"But I can no teach you to turn on the light when the darkness has its hands around your throat. We have to pry its hands off you first. I will to protect you when I can. Sheri and Danny go to your school. They will keep watch on you there. They can no protect you like me but they will do what they can."

This sounded way too good to be true. Nobody does something like this for you without a reason.

"Why would you do this for me?"

"Because it what I do. And because you need it." She put her hand on my shoulder. "I see potential in you, Cohen. I want to explore what you capable of."

I thought about that for a bit. Was she for real? "What can you do?"

"I have . . . abilities . . . skills that most people don't have. And I know people who have abilities. You no believe if I just told you. I must to show you. Is something very few people know about. What are you doing tomorrow?"

"We go to church in the morning. Service is at 11:15. It's over around 12:30. We get lunch, and then usually come back here. My dad falls asleep in front of the TV, usually watching some movie from about 30 years ago, my mother gets grouchy about the house never being clean, and my sister plays in her room. I play my Nintendo or I come out here and play basketball."

"Let's go talk to your parents. I'd like my parents to pick you up tomorrow and take you to Jewish Community Center. There's a . . um . . program we want you to get into."

I had to state the obvious. "I'm not Jewish."

She chuckled. "I know. Your name is, though. And that's close enough for government work . . . hmmm . . . that ironic."

"What's ironic?"

Now she and Amir were both chuckling.

It was clearly an inside joke made at my expense. But somehow it didn't bother me. It probably should have, but these two had just offered me something beyond precious to me. They'd offered me the chance to feel happy again.

Little did I know what else they'd just offered me.

A sane person might have turned them down if he'd known. I wouldn't. I wasn't a sane person. I was a boy lost in the darkness, and they were offering me a light.

CHAPTER TWO – ZIP IT

Tsipporah L. Dagan was born on November 11, 1976 in Haifa, Israel. If you ask her what the "L" stands for, she'll slit your throat. Don't ask me either, cause she's threatened to do worse to any of her friends or family who spill the dark secret of the "L". Her parents named her Tsipporah after the Biblical wife of Moses. Growing up in Haifa, her friends and family all called her "Tsippi" which is a common shortening of her name.

She and her family packed up and immigrated to the United States in the summer of 1984. She'd learned English by the end of the year - primarily from watching TV. But she never quite mastered grammar.

The Dagans lived in the North Dallas area for two years before I ever met them. By then, her new American friends had morphed her nickname from Tsippi to Zippy. She didn't mind. By the time she learned what the word "zipper" meant, the name was firmly entrenched.

My parents had enrolled me in a cotillion ballroom dancing class at Collin Creek Mall when I was 10 years old, completely against my will and much to my utter horror. What boy in his right mind wants to go take a class where he slow dances with girls like he's in some romance film with a bunch of mush? YUCK!!!! But I ended up liking it once I got there. The music was fun and we really did learn how to dance. That's where Zippy and I met.

Zippy was the Middle-Eastern girl with the hook shaped nose and bizarre mop of half-spiked boyish hair sitting on what was otherwise the most serious face you'd ever seen on a kid her age. She was also the girl that all the other boys were afraid to partner with for . . well . . any of the dances. She had a threatening way with her knees, if you get my drift. Not that she'd ever done it, but she could make you think she was going to in a flash, and it scared the hell out of any boy unlucky enough to cross her during the dance lessons.

But for some reason, she seemed to like me, and she never really threatened me or anything. It was as though she'd chosen me out of all the boys to be her friend. I really liked her, but I never saw her outside of the cotillion classes until last year when I found out we lived in the same neighborhood. She went to some private Jewish school in Dallas, and I was firmly planted in the suburbanite hell of the Plano public school system.

Yeah - THAT Plano. Just north of Dallas, it was known as the teen suicide capitol of the world in the mid-1980s. My father had been hired at a major computer company in Dallas so my family chose Plano as our new hometown. I'll say it again, THAT Plano.

THAT Plano is where I met Zippy.

Sunday, March 4, 1990

Even though I'd "known" Zippy for a couple of years, nothing could have prepared me for my introduction to her other world.

When Zippy and I walked into the lounge at the Dallas Jewish Community Center, the other six kids who'd visited my driveway last night were already there.

"Hey hey - Cohen's here!!!!" yelled Danny. They all ran over to meet me. The girls were hugging and the guys were offering handshakes that quickly turned into giant bear hugs. All except Sivan, the eternally depressing Upside-Down Eyelash chick, who I quickly learned was never happy about anything. She gave off this major "there goes the neighborhood" vibe when I walked in.

"Welcome to M-Gang," said Zippy with the biggest smile I'd ever seen on her.

"What's M-Gang?"

She took me by the arm and we began to walk down one of the corridors while the others stayed behind. "That is question which would get some people killed. Is short for MYOP Gang, but nobody ever call it that. The first thing you must know is what you can tell people about us, and what you can't. To your family and everyone at school, say M-Gang is community service program run by Jewish Community Center. It keeps kids like us 'on the right track' by helping with schoolwork and such." She stopped and looked directly in my eyes as though to drive this point home. "This all you can ever tell to anyone." She seemed unusually serious, even for her.

"Okay. My parents will like that, but it also sounds boring as-"

"Is just cover story. The truth is a bit more . . . complicated. M-Gang is sort of a parent-friendly nickname for us." She hesitated for a few seconds, then continued, "The part we don't talk about is . . MYOP stand for Mossad Youth Outreach Program."

She looked at me for a few seconds like this should mean something. When I just stared blankly back at her, she sighed "You have no idea what Mossad is, do you?"

"Is that some sort of secret religious society like Knights of Columbus for Jews?"

She burst out laughing. "Not even close. Oh my

goodness this will be interesting."

We stepped into an empty office-like room with a bunch of abandoned furniture and a phone which wasn't plugged into the wall. Zippy sat on the floor and motioned for me to do the same.

"Mossad is Israeli Intelligence Agency."

"Huh?"

"Is Israel's CIA. M-Gang is a youth recruitment, training . . and soon to be fully field operational division of Israeli CIA."

I had to take a minute to make sure I'd heard her correctly. The words coming out of her mouth sounded utterly insane. "Riiiiiiiiiight. You're a spy, like James Bond or something." I got this sinking feeling like this was some big prank that all the kids at school would be adding to the litany of things to make fun of me for. But the look on her face was dead serious. If this was a prank, she was taking it to the hilt.

She looked at me for what seemed like a very LONG time with that serious face, unflinching. Then she just sighed. "You familiar with the Israeli and Palestinian conflict."

"Yeah . . well, I know about-"

"It was no a question." She sounded a bit impatient. "You familiar because last year a kid in your PE class named Omar told you how terrible WE Israelis were, and even tried to get you to come to fundraiser for Palestinians."

"How did you know about-"

"We know things. The 'charity' group he raising money for is a front for a horrible terrorist organization. That organization is responsible for deaths of many innocent American and Israeli citizens. What exactly did he lead you to believe?"

I had to think for a moment. Omar was a skinny little punk with big round glasses who I'd known in PE class at my last school - did I mention I'd been to three different schools in the last three years? Anyway, when we were on the jogging track, he'd always be going on about how the Israelis did this or the Israelis did that. I wouldn't repeat this to Zippy for fear of annoying her, but I could give her a shortened version. "He said you guys were like bullies. He said you torture his people for no reason."

She snorted. "Figures. Truth is that we in a fight with 'his' people. We no want this fight, but they want to kill us. And they lie. When they kill us, they say is 'resistance' so is okay. But when we kill them, they say is 'oppression' so we evil for doing it. We no want this fight. We want to live. But they rather die trying to kill us than live with us."

"But why? Why would these guys want to kill you?"

She paused. "That is very long story. Did you see that movie on TV last year - War and Remembrance?"

"Yeah - I'll watch anything with Jane Seymour in it. She's hot."

Ooops. I probably shouldn't have said that last part. Zippy sighed, rolled her eyes, and shook her head all at once - "Stupid Texan . . did you see the gas chamber scene?"

"Yeah, I remember it really well. It aired on Tuesday. They did a 'viewer discretion' warning during the commercial, and my mom left the room. Only my dad and I watched it. It was . . .." I couldn't even come up with a word to describe it.

Zippy seemed to just know already, so she continued. "After those things happened, our people all over the world swore 'never again.' This was when we went back to the land that had once been our nation, and we re-took it. The people living there had never formed a nation, but after we re-established Israel, all the other countries in Middle-East say we'd 'stolen' their 'nation' from them, and these countries all declare war on us."

"These are the Palestinians?"

"No. The Palestinians welcome us at first. But other Arabic nations declare war on us. We won. They try again in 1967, but we beat them again. Like I said, 'never again.' They claim they want to 'free the Palestinians,' but they are free in our nation. We even let them to vote. We treat them better than anyone ever treated us. But some people in Middle-East want to make Auschwitz happen again."

"But Omar said they want peace."

"I'm sure they do - their version of it, which means all of my people are dead. Mark, after the last war, the Arab states all declared 'the three no's - no recognition, no negotiation, and no peace.' What can you do to make peace with someone who wants you dead?"

I didn't have an answer. So she provided me with one. "You don't let them make you dead. You fight them and kill them if you have to, and make yourself safe."

She paused for a moment before continuing. "Other nations have made some of the Palestinians to hate us. They have formed many terrorist groups in our nation to try to kill us. The newest group of bad guys is called Hamas. They have motto that they love death more than we love life. They exist just to murder us. Mossad exists to stop them."

"So what does this have to do with you here in Dallas?"

She looked down. "Do you know what happen in 1972?"

"Watergate?"

She shook her head. "Ok, you no know what happen." She looked back up at me. "Palestinian terrorists snuck into Olympics and murder entire Israeli team. It was another test of 'never again'. We had to hit back hard. Mossad sent several teams of assassins on mission called 'Operation: Wrath of God'. They go all over world tracking down and killing everyone who took part in plan. My parents were both part of this mission. That's where they meet and fall in love. They got married and had me. When I was six, they had my little brother, Avi."

She smiled when she mentioned her little brother's name.

"When I was about eight, they re-assigned to USA." She suddenly looked a bit sad. "Another team catch terrorist leader that they had been tracking . . . anyway, it no matter. You want to know how Mossad Youth program came along?"

Ok, now we were getting into the more interesting stuff. "Yeah."

"A few years ago, Mossad director got stupid and sent agent to do secret mission in USA. He got caught. That mess up relationship between Israel and US. It also put my parents at risk. Israelis who were helping US with counter terror work all became suspect. US government got sloppy with protecting us. One of Israel's worst enemies, Iran, sent agents to USA to find and kill Israelis. Iranian agents got to several families and kill them. It was scary time."

Something awful broke through her poker face for a split second. I got the feeling she wasn't just telling me a story, but was letting me in on things she'd experienced firsthand.

"Last year, Mossad got new director - Mr. Shavit. He much smarter than idiot before him. He come up with idea for M-Gang. If terrorist want to kill children of Israeli and American grownups, why not let children join fight against them? He talk with American National Security Agency, and together they come up with idea: recruit American and Israeli children, train us like adult operatives, organize us into teams like Mossad's assassination units, and send us in to do things that would violate international law for adults to do."

"Isn't it illegal to use kids for stuff like that?"

"No exactly. I no entirely sure how it works, but the lawyers say we're good. Our team have no done anything dangerous yet. At first it was just Sivan and me. I did support work on some missions in Israel last summer - that was 'official shakedown run' of M-Gang program. I also recruited most of the other kids myself. Sivan recruited her little brother Amir."

"That's her LITTLE brother??" Muscle guy from yesterday seemed even scarier now.

"Yeah. I used to call him 'pip-squeak.' He really sprouted last year. I recruited Sheri and Danny. They're a couple, you know. And I got Rachael Stein. She is Danny's sister. Then there's Aaron. He also go to my school. He's a lot like you. This summer we're all going to do support work as a team in the Middle-East. Then if everything works, about a year from now we will do live missions on our own."

At this point, I'd given up on the idea that this was a prank. Zippy was either over-the-rainbow bonkers, or this whole thing was for real.

She got up and motioned for me to follow her. She gave me a tour of the facility. There was the standard Jewish Community Center stuff on the first floor. There was even an "M-Gang" lounge for the "community service" group. But unbeknownst to the average visitor, there was a basement - this was the real M-Gang headquarters. The largest room was a huge martial arts gym with punching bags, and two boxes full of equipment - boxing gloves, head-guards, hand-held punching mitts. There was another lounge, this one better equipped with a TV, some couches, a ping-pong table, and some other games. There was also a classroom, where M-Gangers studied the missions of all the counter-terror and defense force agencies in Israel.

We eventually made our way back up to the main lounge. Zippy excused herself to go speak to her parents for a minute or two.

Danny came over to me. "So, what do you think?"

"I think this is crazy . . but it's awesome. So you're a secret agent or something?"

Danny shook his head "Oh no way, man. I'm just a normal seventh-grader like you. We all are . . . well, most of us. Zippy is the real deal. She was the first. She took out an entire Savak wet team all by herself when she was nine years old. But the rest of us just got recruited last summer."

"What's Savak?"

"The Iranian Intelligence Agency. They're scary EVIL people. All of them are assassins - hell, sometimes they even assassinate each other. A few years ago, they sent an undercover team to hunt down and kill Mossad operatives and their families in America."

"Yeah, Zippy was telling me about that stuff - the director getting stupid and a spy getting caught and all that?"

"The Pollard thing, yeah. The spy's name was Pollard. It supposedly got really intense. The Savak team came to Dallas looking for trouble, and they found it alright. Who'd have ever thought a nine-year-old girl would send the whole team packing on a one-way trip to hell?"

"So she killed them? I mean, really KILL killed them?

"Yep."

"Nine years old?"

"Yeah. Just don't ask her about it. She doesn't like to talk about it. I don't know, maybe she feels like it's bragging or something, but she's the toughest chick I know - maybe the toughest in the world. DO NOT piss her off."

"You're not kidding. What about grouchy-face over there?"

"Oh the other Mideastern chick - the one with the weird eyelashes?" Wow, he and I must speak the same language. "That's Sivan Katzav. Don't worry about her. She can't stand me either. In fact, Zippy is about the only person here that she treats like a human being."

"What's her problem?"

"She's Mizrahi - an Iranian Jew. Her parents were expelled in the 70s when the Muslims took over Iran. They immigrated to Israel, but Mizrahi Jews sometimes get mistreated there. It's kinda like how black people were in America during the segregation . . you know, Jim Crow thing. Anyway, Zippy could tell you more about it. She's Mizrahi too, but she doesn't have a chip on her shoulder about it."

I suddenly felt sorry for her. I knew how cruel people could be when they think you're different from them.

Zippy came back from talking to her parents with a huge smile across her face. "My parents have agreed to consider you for the team. So, would you like to join up?"

She reached out and offered me a handshake. It was that scene in Fright Night all over again, and I was Evil Ed. But I didn't take as long to think about it as he did. I had no real friends any more, and Zippy was offering me a kind of acceptance I'd never known. These kids would fight for me . . . well, most of them. I was pretty sure Sivan wouldn't, by the snorting sound she made when I shook Zippy's hand. But as crazy as it sounded, Zippy was also offering me a teenage boy's dream - to be a real live James Bond. What idiot would turn that down?

Zippy was ecstatic, "Awesome. I know is no official yet, but welcome aboard. Now, we need to call your parents, and get them to sit down with my parents. We have to sell this idea to your parents."

"That's going to be a bit hard."

She smirked. "Oh you no worry about that. Suburban parents are simple creatures. They'd sell their souls to hell if it would mean their child make good grades in school. We will help you all we can with this, but we need you to step up in this area. Is the first price you will pay for what we offer. You MUST make good grades in school. If you do this, your parents won't even see the rest. You could probably brag to them of all the throats you slit, and it would go in one ear and out the other, as long as your report card says 'all A grades'."

And that's exactly what happened. The Dagans called my parents and asked if they could meet to discuss a proposition for "setting me straight." Considering the report card I'd brought home a few weeks ago, that wasn't going to be a hard sell. We all headed over to my house.

Zippy agreed to watch "The Little Mermaid" with my sister. I stayed in the dining room with the adults - not that I wanted to, but I was going to beat my head into the wall if I had to listen to that idiotic "wish I could be part of your world" song one more time.

The Dagans talked about how this program of theirs had set several other kids like me "on the right track" and that they could guarantee that I'd make all As in every class with no exceptions. All my parents had to do is let me participate in M-Gang programs Monday through Wednesday evenings, and do occasional weekend programs. They also mentioned an upcoming trip to Israel this summer, and that the program had sponsors who would pay for me to go. All my parents had to do was agree, and then get me a passport. This trip would make me a "changed kid." When the Dagans talked about this great kid I was going to be, you could literally see my parents drooling on the inside.

The Dagans were masters at discovering what would motivate someone, and then pressing that button to the hilt. They left some documents with my dad.

After they left, my dad and I talked for two hours. He wanted to make sure this wasn't just another of my "phases" and that I was serious about this program. It would require me to quit my Tang Soo Do classes, and he was surprised how little this bothered me. I reminded him that there was a martial arts program built into M-Gang. More importantly, M-Gang was completely free.

They were also concerned that M-Gang might try to convert me to Judaism. My dad's side of the family had been Jewish, but my father converted to Catholicism when he married my mom . . at which point his entire family disowned him. And I mean they REALLY disowned him. They didn't just say "you're dead to me." No . . . they held a mock funeral for him and set up a tombstone in a local graveyard with his name on it, listing the date of his conversion as the death-date.

When I was born a few years later, one of my aunts finally broke their silence and swore to him that they'd bring me back into the Hebrew fold no matter what the cost. My dad responded to this by trying to make me super-Catholic. He was always paranoid that his family was somehow plotting to secretly convert me. And now my dad was concerned that the M-Gang might try to convert me as well. But I reminded him of how I couldn't survive without pepperoni pizzas. That settled the issue.

In the end, my parents were desperate for my grades to improve. Zippy was right. Suburban parents aren't complicated at all. All of their arguments, fears, and concerns melted away in face the of this one issue: their son's grades in school. M-Gang guaranteed all A's. My dad shook Jerry Dandridge's proverbial claw almost as quickly as I did. He signed all the papers left by the Dagans. He got them notarized the next day, and I delivered them to Zippy. She said that the other members would vote on me that week, but not to worry – all but one of them wanted me onboard. It didn't take a genius to figure out who the holdout was.

CHAPTER THREE – THE SPIRIT OF HAMAN

Thursday, March 8, 1990

And there I thought with all the hell I'd been getting at school, and with all the prank phone calls I'd been getting at all hours of the day and night, that my classmates had exhausted their interest in me. Stupid me.

I found out otherwise when Alicia Peters, first chair violinist and orchestra teacher's pet, got in my face just before tune-up in orchestra class about "me" prank calling her house last weekend. She'd been home sick all week, so this was the first I was hearing about this. I tried to reason with her, but what was the use? I couldn't convince even ONE of my classmates that the insane stories about me in the bathrooms weren't true. How could I ever hope to convince a raging 12-year old girl that I didn't call her house last Saturday? Besides, what could I tell her? I was busy being recruited by a scary Jewish immigrant into a secret organization that was co-sponsored by the government to employ kids our age as assassins?

Anyway, the upshot was that her big bad daddy was going to "get me" at the violin competition which was scheduled for this coming Saturday. Great, maybe an adult could actually be reasoned with . . . right?

That night, the phone rang. A rather annoyed Zippy was on the line.

"How am I to protect you if you no tell me when someone threaten you?

"Huh?"

"Sheri saw the whole thing in orchestra class. This girl's father threaten to hurt you. No on my watch!!! When this competition thing? I will be there."

Oh boy, there it was again - that sinking feeling. The thought of Zippy seeing me with that ridiculous violin case slung over my shoulder made me want to crawl off into a corner and die!!! But then again, she was right. How could she be my guardian angel if she wasn't there when someone threatened to hurt me? Hmmm . . . the danger of Alicia's father actually being there and wanting to kill me versus the humiliation of the Zippy seeing me with the violin. Not so tough a choice, really . . .

"I'm sorry, but you can't be there. It's Saturday morning. You're going to be in your synagogue for Saturday service."

After a long pause, I could hear her and her mother shouting back and forth in Hebrew. Then suddenly she was back with "Is no problem. I meet you Saturday at your house."

Yep, that was me - crawling off into a corner. This was so going to suck!!!!!

Saturday, March 10, 1990

And with military punctuality, Zippy's mom dropped her off at my house, along with her little brother Avi, dressed to the nines in their Shabbat wear. They'd just come from her Synagogue, splitting right after the Torah reading when nobody was looking.

"Hang on a minute, you guys all just left in the middle of the service?"

"Uh . . yes." Zippy replied.

"I thought you guys were totally into the religion thing?"

"Mark, protecting someone like you is what we Jews consider viable charity work. Is important to God that you do things for people who need help - people like you."

"I didn't know that Jews bought into the whole 'golden rule' thing."

"It was Jew who invented it. Anyway, I'd like to hear you play your violin."

"That's cause you've never heard me play it."

She snorted before going off to say hi to my mom and Elise, who were racing out the door to go to a Brownies meeting.

My dad drove us all to the competition over at Plano Senior High, promising to return in two hours flat. It was one of those completely grey days - perpetually threatening to storm like crazy, but only a couple of raindrops actually fell out of the sky.

I played my assigned violin piece from memory, then began the hour-long wait for the judges to post results. Less that fifteen minutes later, I found myself face-to face with a short man in his mid-40s. He had a big bald patch right in the middle of his head, and a mustache that made him look like a cross between a biker and a cop.

"Excuse me, do you know which of these kids is Mark Cohen?"

"Yeah, that's me."

Have you ever seen someone's face turn bright red over the course of ONE sentence? "I'm Alicia Peters's father, and I got a message on my answering machine from you the other night that you'd gone and made out with her in the back of a car. That's my daughter you were talking about!!!"

"Well, you know it wasn't me, right? I never called your house. Why would someone prank call you and leave their own name, that would be-"

"Oh that's real cute!" He got right up in my face . . so much for reason. "Listen here you little punk!! If you ever call my house again I'm going to give your parents a choice: we can either let the police handle it or let me handle it. And I'd much rather they let me handle it cause I'm going to enjoy it a hell of a lot better and-"

"Excuse me." Zippy's voice was so soft it sounded almost baby-like. I hadn't even noticed her coming up behind me, placing her hand on my right shoulder and slowly scooting me back, edging her way in between me and the angry shouting half-bald guy. "This boy never made any phone calls to your house."

The guy just stood there for a second. He started pointing his finger at Zippy's face. "You best run along before you get into trouble, too. This here's between me and this little-"

"Oh is much too late for that. And there's nothing between you and Mark but me. And I will always be standing right here - between Mark and pathetic old bags like you."

Ever see a grown man's jaw drop? Zippy quickly leaned in so that nobody around us would hear, whispering, "and if you ever threaten my friend again, I make you cry in front of your pretty little wife and daughter."

The words danced out of her mouth with an almost poetic softness. She sounded like she was reading him a love letter. I'd seen Zippy threaten boys before, but I'd never seen this. Usually she'd have a playful look on her face, but in this brief moment, she was a predator. She looked like a hungry toddler staring at birthday cake. Her eyes glazed over like she was intentionally blurring her vision. She was staring at his throat. The rest of her entire body relaxed into this un-natural calm.

Maybe it was having his self-righteous rant derailed. Maybe it was being threatened. Maybe it was just an ego that couldn't take having a girl get in his face. But you could see the rage explode across his already furious face. His right hand grabbed Zippy by the lapel.

In a flash, Zippy's right hand came across her chest, grabbing his hand on her lapel. Her left hand came to his elbow, and her right leg lashed like a bullwhip right up in between his legs. This all happened simultaneously in one lightning-fast blur. His whole body jolted, and she immediately had him in some scary looking ninja arm lock, from which she promptly threw him head-first into the wall.

"Don't touch me!!!! Somebody help!!!" she screamed.

I didn't understand this yet, but one of the most powerful tools in a female operative's toolbox is the ability to summon knights in shining armor by pretending that a male target is trying to hurt her.

In this case, a bunch of very large guys were surrounding Mr. Peters in a matter of seconds.

"This man touched my breast" she said, in a voice so shaky even I nearly believed it. And apparently, from the angle most of the bystanders had, it looked like just that when he grabbed her lapel. So after spinning a tale of the big bad evil pervert guy, and how she knew what to do from a "self-defense seminar" her mother had forced her to take (augmented by Mr. Peters writhing on the ground, clutching his damaged groin), Zippy managed to turn a scary moment for me into an object lesson in situation control.

Mr. Peters couldn't get much sympathy from the crowd, and ended up just settling for "it was all a big misunderstanding" before high-tailing it out of there with his family in tow.

Avi had watched the entire show from across the hall. He'd probably seen his sister do stuff like this before.

Fortunately, nobody called the police, so we weren't stuck there all day. Instead, we were only stuck there the minor eternity that it took for the competition results to post. I'd completely blown it. The only way it would have been worse would be if they'd stamped "YOU SUCK" across the results.

My father showed up after everything had died down. He wasn't happy with my performance, but hey - I HATED the violin. Maybe he'd figure that out eventually. He knew nothing of the incident until months later. Zippy and I didn't discuss it with each other till we got back to my house, and had some privacy out in my back yard.

"I normally no would have handled it that way." She seemed a little embarrassed for showing off in front of me. "I'm normally brilliant with defusing situations like that. I could have convinced to him of your innocence and even had him apologizing to you. If I really wanted, I could to have him trying to persuade you to date his precious Alicia."

"Oh vomit!"

"Admit it. You think she's cute." Zippy was in her full 'teasing girl' mode, and I knew that it'd only get worse if I continued to deny . . . but this was a line I couldn't cross.

"Never."

"Hmmmm . . . Interesting. Anyway, I took different route for your sake."

"For me? You beat up Alicia's dad so I could see you fight?

"Mark!!!!" She feigned shock. "I'm insulted. That no was fight. There was no ambulance, no hearse . . . no even any blood. No. I do that because that man believe a lie about you, and he was going to hurt to you because of the lie he believe. Too many people hurt you over lies, and I thought you needed to see at least one person pay for doing this."

Later that evening, Zippy's family invited me to their

Synagogue for a special Jewish holiday service called Purim. It was an absolute blast. The Rabbi got up and read a book out of the Old Testament, while the congregation acted like they were watching the Rocky Horror Picture Show. I'm not kidding. They booed and hissed whenever the Rabbi mentioned the bad guy's name. They'd cheer wildly whenever he'd say the good guy's name. Various people would take turns throwing candy into the crowd. People danced in the isle.

Zippy really got into it. She went absolutely nuts whenever the Rabbi said the name "Mordecai." He was the "good guy" in the story the Rabbi read. And I thought she was going to pull out a gun whenever the Rabbi said "Haman." You can figure out who he was. I asked her about it afterwards, something she totally wasn't expecting.

"Seriously Mark, I knew I'd be to teach to you how to fight, use a gun, and survive in any situation you ever end up in, but I never thought I teach to you basic Judaism."

We were sitting in a corner in one of the classrooms at her temple. We had a plate full of cookies we'd snagged from the temple's kitchen area right after service.

"Sorry. They didn't cover this stuff in Catechism."

"I know. I'm just a little more used to solving problems that I can hit, kick, or shoot than dealing with this. Mark, you're a descendant of the Cohanim. Is in your last name: Cohen. You Jewish, even if you no practice Judaism."

"Ok, so tell me about going nuts over the guy's name. I thought you were going to take a baseball bat to the Rabbi if he said that name again." I wasn't going to dare utter the name. She might tear my throat out or something.

She sighed, and after a long pause, began with "Haman was no the first, and he was no the last, but he was major link in chain of people who tried to exterminate my people. They all fail. Throughout the ages, my people have been persecuted in every nation where we ever existed. But that's life when you're a Jew. Someone always trying to kill us."

She said it almost with a shrug. I don't think I could take someone trying to send me to meet my maker so lightly. She downed another cookie, then continued, "When someone becomes powerful and uses their powerful position to try to murder Jews, we call them 'Agagite.' Haman was Agagite. Although now there's one even more famous than him."

I had to think for a minute. "Hitler?"

"No other. We Jews never forget that there is powerful spirit out there who want to destroy us. We remember this every year on Purim holiday. We also remember that God will protect us, and that each of us may have been born for just one moment where we risk it all to save many."

"So this is what M-Gang does too?"

"Yes. We prepare ourselves for that moment where any one of us may need to risk it all to do great things. There are terrible people planning terrible things at this very moment. Most people think they're safe because they no see danger in their daily lives. But the danger is there. This is why we do what we do."

"You're trying to be Hadassah?"

"No." She picked up another one of the cookies we'd snagged, but only took a nibble. "I only trying to be prepared in case life puts me in place where I have to do something myself. We all have talents. I just discovered mine at early age. Unlike most girls, I have talent for quickly winning physical confrontations . . . speaking of which, can you come down to M-Gang training center tomorrow afternoon?"

"Uh . . . sure. What's up?"

"I did no tell you??? The team voted. You're in. You're the eighth member of M-Gang inaugural unit. So I need to train you."

"Train me in what?

"Well, I can no be your personal bodyguard forever, so

I'm going to make you indestructible. Would you like to have my fighting skills?"

"Yes, but I've been taking Karate for 2 years, and gotten nowhere. Skills like yours take years. I don't kn-"

"Mark. First of all, what form of Karate do you know?"

"Tang Soo Do."

She burst out laughing so hard that she choked.

"Wow. Korean dance fighting? No wonder you get beaten up all the time. I bet you look real cute doing choreographed fights while wearing pajamas. You might even get to show off your skills by breaking boards."

"Yeah. I'm good at br-"

"What good does this do to you? So what if you can break stationary board? Have you gotten into confrontation with stationary board lately?"

I just sat there. I didn't really have a response.

"I did no think so. I will teach you what I know. I have advanced training in Krav Maga, K-PAP and Hisardut. The first two are essentially Israeli Ninjitsu, and Hisardut is Israeli Jujitsu. This I will teach to you. I asked Sivan to help, but she refused. So I asked her brother instead. Amir said yes immediately."

She downed another cookie, "Just do no show up wearing some ridiculous pajama uniform," she started to laugh as she pointed her finger right at my face, "because then I will to hurt you."

"What should I wear then?

She shrugged. "What you always wear. T-shirt, shorts, tennis shoes. We already went to sports store and bought everything else you need."

"Like what?"

"You'll see." That evil smile crept across her face.

We were down to the last of the cookies. She grabbed it before I could blink.

CHAPTER FOUR – ISRAELI NINJITSU

Oh I found out alright. I showed up the next day at M-Gang, wearing my T-shirt, shorts, and tennis shoes. Sure enough, they'd bought me some equipment - a mouthguard, compression shorts, and a CUP!!!! A friggen CUP!!! Do you have ANY idea how humiliating it is to have a girl buy you a cup????

Zippy wouldn't let me walk into the training room unless I was wearing it. I'd never worn one in Karate cause we almost never sparred. It was so embarrassing - the first time I tried to put one on, I put it on UPSIDE DOWN. Zippy and Amir both exploded laughing when they saw the . . . um . . . bulge it made. It took them a few minutes to regain composure and explain just how the stupid things are supposed to go on.

How was I to know? I'd never done sports. There are some things people just take for granted that you know, and they tell you to just do it. Like all the idiot PE coaches who react to your inability to do a proper pushup by trying to make you do more pushups. But my new friends weren't like that. They'd laugh but they'd help.

The training couldn't have been further from my

experience in Karate. There were no uniforms, no belts, no meditation, and no bowing. We all wore shorts, sweats, t-shirts, and tennis shoes. And Zippy had a boom-box blaring out various metal albums the whole time. My Tang Soo Do instructors would be horrified.

Zippy started the first lesson in a rather abrupt manner. "I no interested in stances. You will only know two stances. One is just standing there, feet apart at width of your shoulders, hands at your side. This is 'you are no fighting' stance. The other looks like this," she stepped forward and put her hands up in front of her. "This is 'you are fighting' stance."

I thought I had the stance right, but she still came over and moved my hands out a bit further.

"Hands too close can no deflect incoming punch. Hands too far out get grabbed, and this will suck for you. Now . . . RELAX SHOULDERS!!!!!!"

You'd think having someone suddenly scream at your face would make you do anything BUT relax, but Zippy had a way about her. She was always telling me to relax because you can't fight with your muscles tensed up.

"Ok, now you learn how to move." She spent the next ten minutes teaching me to walk without ever crossing my legs. I felt very clumsy, but she insisted that I was doing okay. "If you no end up in good stance, FIX it. This is not Karate. This is fight. You no being graded on perfection here - only on winning. Now . . you look like you have a question."

"Uh . . yes I do."

"Then why you no ask it?"

"Because I'm not supposed to question techni-."

SMACK!!!!! She'd slapped me!!!!! She friggen SLAPPED me!!!!!!!

"You here to learn! How you learn if you no ask when something make no sense?"

From then on, I became the most inquisitive student in

the history of martial arts.

I thought I knew how to throw a punch. You make your hand into a ball and launch it into the other person, right? Apparently, this was wrong. Zippy taught me a whole new way to punch, using my entire body to launch my hand into the target like a whip.

"Keep your elbows in!!!!!!"

I cringed. It didn't make any sense to do that, so I needed to ask why. In a traditional martial arts class, you'd be doing pushups for this, but . . .

"Why?"

Zippy stepped right in front of me and pointed her finger right at my nose.

"Follow my finger with your eyes."

She began moving it from side to side, then brought it back to center, still pointing at my nose.

"Easy, no?"

"Yeah."

"Do it again."

Without warning, her finger shot forward and tapped me HARD on the nose.

"Eyes detect side to side motion long before they detect incoming motion. If elbows stay in, your enemy will no see punch till is too late. Now, let's do it for real."

For real?!?!? Yep, next thing I knew, Amir was standing by me with a hand held punching bag.

"I am no interested in seeing you punch air. You no punch air in fight. You punch target."

You just couldn't argue with her.

She made me punch the bag with each hand. She made me do left/right combinations. And I had to finish with a thirty second drill called "kill the bag," where I had to just keep hitting as hard and fast as I could. Zippy taught me more in the first 8 minutes of our lesson together than I had learned in two years of Tang Soo Do.

"I could teach you all of the different places on the face

to strike, but in real fight this is useless. You always punch to the face or throat, and hit whatever you manage to hit. In real confrontation, trying to precision aim is stupid."

She had me do "kill the bag" for a little longer. I thought this was all we were going to cover, when she suddenly asked an odd question.

"You are boy. What hurts worse: getting kicked in the balls, or getting kneed in the balls."

Well, I'd been kicked before, but managed to avoid every boy's worst nightmare, the knee, up to this point. Oddly enough, Amir reflexively chimed in with me, and we said it in unison, "kneed."

She smiled a bit, "Good answer, boys. Amir, let Mark try to figure out this. Why does it hurt worse?"

"I don't know. It just does more damage?"

"Yes, but why?"

I paused for a moment, "I really don't know."

"Is fine. Physics can wait for another day. The important part is that you're right. Knees destroy everything in their path. Same for elbows. They destroy everything they touch. So striking with elbow will always hurt more than striking with fist."

And with that, she began working me through various elbow strikes. I was having so much fun that I didn't realize just how much time had passed, or how insanely I was starting to sweat. We took a fifteen minute break, and Zippy went to call Rachael. She was trying to arrange an all M-Gang sleepover during spring break, and the Steins still hadn't agreed to a specific date.

I asked Amir if she had done this training routine with all the kids.

"Not really. She taught me and my sister, but that was a long time ago. Now, most of the kids in M-Gang train together. Tsipporah and Sivan usually teach together." I was really unaccustomed to hearing anyone call Zippy by her birth name. "My sister is almost up there at

Tsipporah's skill level, but not quite. The only other kid who ever got private training was Aaron."

"Why him?"

"He's like you. He was beat up by bullies. Tsipporah found out about it cause he went to D'var Adonai." D'var Adonai was the private Jewish school where most of the M-Gang kids attended - Zippy included. "There were some kids in his neighborhood who went to that church over by the mall."

"Our Lady of the Sacred Tears?"

"You know it?"

Oh, I knew it alright. My parents went there briefly after we first moved to Plano. It had a display by its front door which looked like a box of sand with a bunch of candles in it. One day I got fed up and called the church "Our Lady of the Sacred Cat-box" in front of a couple of the nuns. We found a new church the next week.

He continued, "Well these kids went to that church, and they caught Aaron after their service one Saturday night and beat him up pretty badly. They said that he killed Jesus."

It was hard for me to imagine anyone messing with Aaron, but who knows what he'd been like last year. Maybe in a year, I'd be just like him - fearless.

Zippy returned, and we started working on the lower body - a detail I was thankful for since my arms felt like they were about to break off at the shoulders.

Zippy began in her usual 'no introductions" manner. "In Israel, we do no make flying, spinning, dance kicks. That . . . crap! We have a few of basic kicks, and this is all. I teach you just one today. Is the most useful, the one to the groin."

Amir took the punching shield with both hands, and bent over, holding it in front of himself, just about knee level.

BAM!!! She'd kicked the shield so hard it lifted Amir off the ground. BAM BAM BAM!!!!!! Each one of those kicks were so hard, so fast, and made such a loud noise that I'd jump instinctively. Each one would have dropped any man, and probably sent him to the hospital. These weren't the types of kicks I'd seen before. These were BRUTAL, vicious, scary . . I don't even have the words. And they came so rapid fire that I don't think anyone could ever slump over, or fall to the ground quickly enough to stop her from landing two or three.

"Gooooood God!!!!!!!!!" I gasped.

"Would you like to see it again?

Amir readjusted the death grip he had on the punching shield, bent over again and . . . BAM BAM BAM BAM!!!!!!

"I never just rack. I break. If I kick once, and it doesn't rupture the organs, then I did no kick hard enough. You understand? We're not playing around. I never just kick someone because I think is funny. If I kick to you, is no different than shooting you with gun. You never shoot someone unless you intend to kill them. You never rack someone unless you intend to completely destroy him. You understand?"

I just nodded. I was afraid that if I tried to speak, a squeaking noise would be all I could muster.

Next, she walked me through the mechanics of the kick. But when I tried it for real against the punching shield, it felt SO weak. It was like I was barely tapping it compared to Zippy's murderous barrage. Still, I hit it as hard as I could. When she made me do a "kill the bag" drill where I had to kick it nonstop, I honestly felt like the shots were getting harder . . even though I nearly collapsed from exhaustion afterwards.

Finally, there were knee strikes. I'd been wondering what scary addition she had to make to these. And as had been the case all afternoon, Zippy did not disappoint. She seemed to lock onto the side of Amir's body like some predatory snake, choking the life from its prey. And when she drove her knee up, her entire body see-sawed upwards into the pad. She kneed the pad so hard that it BLASTED his entire body off the ground.

"Like I say earlier, knees destroy everything they hit. They no precision weapons. They like the H-bomb. They no need to be precise. Aim for the groin. If you hit it, great. If you miss it, no problem. You'll still REALLY hurt opponent no matter where you hit him."

She went on to show me how to lock up on the bad guy, which is easy to do, but hard to describe. Then you shoot your hips forward and your knee up. When I tried it, I hit the pad, but it hurt my knee. That's how hard I was hitting. I could barely imagine how bad it would be for the person receiving that shot.

"Ok, that all for techniques. We start every lesson by practicing every technique against pad. And every lesson, we will work on one self-defense technique. Today, I will show you how to break out of choke. Ok, come choke me and I teach you."

This was when I realized why they bought me a cup. When Zippy demonstrated techniques on me, she'd never hit me directly in the face. She'd always punch to the side and miss my cheek by about a half inch. But everything below the throat was fair game. My ribs and arms got bruised up pretty badly. And when she'd get me in the cup, it felt like I wasn't even wearing it. That's right, she kicked so hard she could literally rack me THROUGH the cup. She claimed she was taking a little bit of strength off the kick so as to not hurt me, but you sure could have fooled me on that one.

We went over so much in that first lesson I didn't think I'd have a prayer of remembering it. But the next day we warmed up by reviewing every single technique. Each of us took turns hitting the bags with each technique. I actually started picking it all up by about the fourth or fifth lesson.

She also taught me how to repel attacks. There are basically 6 different ways someone can attack you unarmed:

strikes, chokes, bear-hugs, grabs, headlocks, and what Zippy called "that stupid Jujitsu wrestler wants to roll around and play on the ground." But the defenses were all virtually the same: address the danger and simultaneously counter-strike. Then, as Zippy was fond of saying, "Destroy them. Repeated knees and kicks to groin, with elbows and head-buts thrown in for good measure till your enemy is dead, dying, or wishing he was dead. Do never to stop!"

She also taught me a few "finishing techniques" for ending someone's ability to fight you after you've "softened him up" during the "destroying them" phase. A couple of those techniques scared me because they were lethal. She showed me several different ways to snap someone's neck. The moves were deceptively gentle, right up to the moment she'd violently wrench the head.

The non-lethal "finishing" techniques all involved breaking bones - typically the kneecap. She was big on "taking someone's mobility away." Of course, by the time she got to that "finishing" point, she'd have crushed his privates into mush, gouged out an eye or two, broken his nose, broken his jaw, and probably given him a concussion, so I didn't see much use in taking the mobility, but she insisted that this was key to ending a fight.

After I learning how to get out of a choke-hold on that first day, I asked her what she was going to teach me the next day.

"You will review choke, because you will suck at it by this time tomorrow. You have to practice these things many times before they become natural. I will also teach to you what to do when someone point gun at your face?"

"Huh?" I couldn't have possibly heard her correctly.

"Defense against handgun pointed at your face." She said it with such nonchalance, she sounded downright bored.

"Um, using a real gun?" Part of me knew the answer already.

"Yes. What, do you think I waste your time with a toy or something. No worry, it will no to be loaded."

Gee, that's a comfort.

I thought of all the times I'd been beaten up in school, and all these new things I was learning, and I knew it wouldn't be long until I could live by the words, "Never Again!" But that wasn't going to come around just yet. After each lesson, she'd warn me not to try using any of this at school just yet, because overconfidence gets people killed at the early phases of training.

CHAPTER FIVE – TO DANCE OR TO FIGHT

Outside of M-Gang, my life was turning out to be as problematic as ever, particularly in orchestra class. After the violin competition, Alicia's behavior towards me darkened significantly. She used to make fun of me, gloat at me whenever I'd do badly in one of our weekly class challenges, and taunt me. Now, she was in full cruelty mode and everyone in the class knew there was pure hatred between us. At one point, Sheri and Danny even pulled her aside and swore to her that it wasn't me who made the prank call to her house, but she wouldn't listen. She didn't want to hear it.

Then on a really miserable Wednesday, her sheet music went missing. Every kid in the class insisted that I must have been the one who stole it. As fate would have it, this was also on a day that our regular teacher was out sick. We had a sub, and she believed every word of it. She made me get up and "look" for Alicia's sheet music while the rest of the class watched. She was one of those grouchy ladies who was only teaching for the paycheck. And, like many

Plano teachers, she seemed to have a grudge against all male students. Sheri risked getting a detention by standing up for me and helping "search" for Alicia's sheet music. She ended up finding it behind the trophies in a back corner of the room.

When our actual teacher returned, she scolded the entire class for blaming me without any proof or reason. As it turned out, Jeremy Smith was the culprit. He was the overweight kid with gigantic round glasses who sat in the back of the class. He used his faux "self-esteem due to weight" issues to excuse treating everyone around him like crap. He'd beaten me up twice since the rumors started. I was not surprised to find that he was the one behind the theft. He didn't even have a problem with Alicia. He just did it to her because he knew the class would blame me.

Monday April 2nd, 1990

Spring break came around quickly. I'd spent so much time with Zippy that you'd think we'd get sick of each other, but when we both got a week off from school, all I wanted to do was spend every minute with my new best friend. We'd spend an hour in the morning and an hour in the evening doing Krav Maga training. In between, we watched movies, spent time with other M-Gangers at the pool in Zippy's back yard, and played games. We even got our siblings involved. Zippy's little brother Avi was quite the card shark. And Zippy spent plenty of time with my sister Elise, playing dolls and doing other girlie stuff. For some reason, Zippy became rather attached to Elise.

My mom dropped me off at the Dagan house early in the morning. We spent an hour in their pool, then got changed and were off to lunch. Mrs. Dagan dropped Zippy and me off at an Italian restaurant outside of Collin Creek Mall called Campari's.

On our way in, we spotted a VERY beat-up old car. It

was an Oldsmobile from a few decades ago, and it had a bumper sticker on it which said "I like your Christ, I do not like your Christians. Your Christians are so unlike your Christ. ~Mahatma Gandhi."

Zippy snorted, "He has no idea how right he is."

I asked what she meant, and she said "Jesus was Israeli, like me. He was Jew, like me." We'd made our way to the hostess. "Could we get a table for two, please?"

After we'd been seated, she continued "Is impossible to understand Jesus unless you think like an Israeli, and I do no see ANY Christians who ever been able to think like us."

"But I thought Jews didn't like Jesus."

"Jews in America do no like him. But you know how I feel about that. Most of them would hardly qualify as Jewish in my book. Many of them could no even recite our prayers like Shema without having them written down in front of them - in ENGLISH letters. If you can no recite the prayers from memory and read Hebrew, then you are NO a Jew to me."

She picked up a crayon and started writing something in Hebrew on the paper table-cloth. Campari's always supplied each table with crayons, and their tablecloths were made of paper, so you could write all over them. I loved this place.

"But as for Jesus . . . in Israel, we think of Jesus as sort of 'hometown boy makes good.' You understand the idea of 'hometown hero' - the famous guy who was born here and such. Jesus is most famous Israeli in history. He single-handedly keeps tourism industry in my country going. Why would we no like him? We make fortune off of him."

She had to stop there. A waiter was coming over to take our order, which was really simple. We both wanted bowls of Minestrone, and we wanted to split an order of ravioli with artichoke hearts and lemon butter sauce.

We got sidetracked from our discussion of religion for a few minutes while we played hangman on the table. After the waiter brought our soup, I had to ask her a little more about the religion thing.

"I thought you guys blamed Jesus for all the stuff that happened to you, like those guys who beat up Aaron and called him 'Christ-killer', and-"

"This exactly what I mean. Jesus is our blood relative. He Israeli. We can no blame him when idiots take his message and twist it. They can no even get his life story correct. Do you think he really born on December 25th?"

I shook my head yes.

"Here is hint for you - Israelis went by lunar calendar. The month of December did no exist for us.

"So where do we get Christmas?"

"Pagan festival with wreathes and trees and such in Rome. They just assign his birth date to fit the festivals they already celebrating."

"Wow. Where'd you learn this stuff?"

"Read a history book, Mark." She looked from side to side to make sure nobody was looking, then picked up the bowl and drank it in one gulp.

"Nice trick." I couldn't help but chuckle.

"Thanks. So really, I'm cool with Christianity, although I find some of customs a little weird, and a few of the songs seem insane to me."

"Like which ones?"

"There's this one you sing around Christmas called 'Little Town of Bethlehem' that I don't get. Why would anyone write ode to Bethlehem? I've been there. Is dump."

"Well . . . Jesus was born there."

"Yes, but he no stay there. You notice he got out as quickly as he could. That's another way that Christians are nothing like Jesus. He would never sing ode to Bethlehem. The only ode anyone sing to Bethlehem is 'Dear Lord, please get me the hell out of here in one piece.' Wretched city!!! The whole West Bank is dreadful, and Bethlehem is right in middle of it. He went up north to live in Nat Zaret . . . sorry, Nazareth."

"Are these places that we're going to see while we're in Israel?" I was still hoping that my passport would come in time. Everyone was fairly certain that I was going to be onboard for the big M-Gang Israel trip this summer.

"I hope not," she replied. "I like staying in coastal cities. They fun. Tel Aviv is great. Haifa is AWESOME. But Nazareth is too close to Lebanon for me. Is right up in middle of the northern territory. And Bethlehem is just terrible place. You should want to skip them both."

I finished my soup, "I'd like to skip them, but I've gotta tell my parents I visited SOME Christian sites. My dad is paranoid about you guys converting me to Judaism."

She burst out laughing, "We Jews are no big on converting people. You either born Jewish, or you no Jewish. There are exceptions like you. Your last name betrays you, Cohen. Your family is Jewish, but you no practice Judaism. So some Rabbis would probably take a shot at converting you."

She snorted. "Me, on the other hand - they probably wish I never came around. Many Rabbis feel like Judaism is a worse place to be with people like me in the neighborhood."

That comment made even less sense, so I had to ask "What's that supposed to mean?"

"I'm Mizrahi. My father was Iranian Jew who moved to Israel when he was little boy. Sivan is also. Both her parents were Iranian Jews."

"Yeah. Danny told me about this."

She looked shocked. That was a first. "So you know about Mizrahim and the things we sometimes to deal with. My mother was Sephardic. So when they get married they have 'screw you' attitude to whole world. Is why nobody mess with them."

We paid out, then walked across the parking lot to the mall, where we hung out at a record store waiting for Mrs. Dagan and Avi to show up and take us home. I really loved hanging out with Zippy. Every second I spent with her made me feel lucky to be there. Here's the coolest girl on the planet, and yeah that's right, she's with ME!!!

That night, the entire M-Gang team had a sleepover at the Dagan house. I finally got to see Zippy's room. She had posters of her two favorite bands hanging: Def Leppard and Depeche Mode. There was also this picture of a GORGEOUS Mid-Eastern chick. I asked who the hot one was.

"Oh, is Ofra Haza. She most famous singer in Israel - more famous than Madonna even. Her 'Shaday' album is one of those tapes that everyone just has to own. I love her. She awesome!!! Then there's Depressed Mode. I listen to them when I'm mad" she said, pointing at the dark picture of the four grumpy British guys with the spiked hair. Then she pointed at the metal band. "And over there is Def Leppard. Their 'Hysteria' album is most important heavy metal album ever made."

"I see you haven't got any Cure."

"Nah – too dreary, but Sivan loves them. I will make an Ofra Haza fan of you," she said pointing her finger at me mischievously.

That evening was one of the best in my life. We played board games. We danced around, occasionally lip-synching and air-guitaring to some of the music.

Zippy put on that 'Shaday' album by the Israeli singer. She and Sivan started dancing in the middle of the room, like they both knew every move from a video. They both sang along "Yah know I love yah like no uthah, like no uthah, hear mah praaaaaer." It was great. By the end of the song, we were all up and dancing. The second track was going "Eshaaaaal, stay with us tonight, to dance not to fight" which seemed oddly appropriate for the evening's festivities.

Eventually, Mrs. Dagan came in shouting "Enough already!!!! Turn it off." So we killed the music, and spent the rest of the night watching movies. We decided to watch some horror movies, so we put in The Omen and Salem's Lot. We all dozed off at some point.

We spent the next couple of days of spring break hanging out together, until everyone in the gang started heading off to different towns to visit different relatives. In my case, it came on Thursday.

My family and I piled into a car and headed out to visit my mom's parents. While my dad's parents may have gone to their graves without ever speaking another word to him (or to me for that matter), my mom's parents were the exact opposite.

I spent a few very happy days there playing various games with my sister in the back yard, and listening to a new tape my grandparents had bought for me, Pete Townshend's "All the Best Cowboys Have Chinese Eyes." It felt like pop music for a funeral.

Listening to it on our drive back, I had this terrible feeling of doom, like going back to school was going to be horrible as soon as Monday morning rolled around. It had just been too many days since I'd had a REALLY bad day. I was worried. As I was about to find out, I had every reason to be.

CHAPTER SIX – NO ALIBIS

Monday April 23, 1990

I just had this feeling of doom from the moment my dad dropped me off at school. Something was really off. When I got to my second period English class, I found out what. An announcement came over the PA system, summoning me to the office.

When I got to the office, there was Principle Samson, the Dean of Students/Discipline guy - Mr. Williams, two female Plano Police officers, and . . . Mr. Peters.

My heart sank. I immediately knew what had happened. And I knew that they'd already decided that I did it. Nothing I could say would change that. We all went into a meeting room behind closed doors. Mr. Peters was so mad that he looked like he was about to burst.

The first thing the school did was try to call my parents - who were thankfully both away from their jobs this morning. I mentioned that they'd left the Dagans in charge of me in their absence. Sure enough, the school had put that bit in my student file just last week. It had been one of the steps that Mr. Dagan suggested for helping the program "set me straight."

The secretary called the Dagans and gave them a whole line of nonsense about how I was in trouble for making prank calls to some girl's house. When she hung up, she turned and said "They're on their way over."

The cops took over from there. "I'm Officer Brown. This is Officer Keating. We're here because Mr. Peters says you've been making prank calls to his house. Do you have anything to say for yourself?"

Well, it didn't work with Mr. Peters, but I guessed there wasn't any harm in trying the honest approach. "I never made any prank calls to anyone." Mr. Peters blew up. "See, that's the same crap he tried with me!!! This little punk needs-"

"Mr. Peters, please." The cop gestured for him to calm down before looking back at me. "Son, everyone says they didn't do it, but we've got you on tape." They put a little tape player down in front of me.

There was a knock at the door. Mrs. Peters was there, along with Alicia. They were carrying a little white gadget. I had no idea what it was.

The cop made me sit down, then she hit the play button. This was obviously a tape from an answering machine. A voice that any idiot could tell wasn't mine started up right after the beep, " Huh - this is Mark Cohen from school. I just wanted to tell Alicia how hot she is and how she was the total slut making out with me in the back of my mom's car last night." Alicia looked absolutely disgusted, like she was about to cry. She lunged across the room at me and SMACK - she slapped me across the face so hard it spun my head to the side. I was SO glad I'd worn the wax on my braces.

But there was a huge lump growing in my throat. Being slapped across the face will do that to you - especially when you have no recourse, and everyone is watching and thinking you deserved it. The cops hadn't even tried to stop her. They just put their hands up and said not to do it again, before turning back on me.

"Well what do you have to say for yourself?" The cop sounded like she actually thought I'd confess. I didn't want to say anything. I wanted to sit there quietly. I knew if I opened my mouth, I'd start crying. But I also knew that nothing I said would be believed. They'd assume anything was a lie. Where the hell were the Dagans??

"Well?????" She wasn't going to let it go. I looked around. Pure hatred burned in Alicia's eyes . . same with her dad. The other adults were looking at me like I was some sort of criminal who'd just been caught.

I gulped, clinched my fists, and whispered out the words "That's not me."

Mr. Peters threw his hands in the air. Principal Samson let out an annoyed sigh and shook her head. The officer just stood there staring at me. After a few seconds of murmuring among the adults about "that kid" and how "he just needed" this or that, as though I wasn't in the room, the cop went over to Mrs. Peters and took the little white gadget from her. She found an outlet in the wall and plugged it in, then started pressing buttons on it.

"This is called a 'caller ID box.' We loan these out to stalking victims and victims of prank calls. It records incoming phone numbers and the exact time that a call comes in." She set it on the table in front of me and crossed her arms.

She looked at me with an absolute gloat in her eyes. A victorious smirk crept onto her face. "Recognize that number?"

I looked at it. The little screen on the box looked like an overgrown digital watch. It was flashing "972-555-4197." It could have been anyone's phone number. I didn't know it. "No."

"Don't make this even harder on yourself. The judge is going to decide whether you go to Juvenile Hall or not and how long you spend there, based on what I tell him."

"I don't know that number." I was trying to keep calm.

"That's YOUR phone number, Mark Cohen!!!"

I shook my head using as little motion as possible. I didn't want to piss her off worse. "My number is 972-555-7608. I don't know this number."

She just stood there exasperated. I didn't want to wait and give her a chance to say the words "you're under arrest" so I volunteered whatever proof I could. "Check the student directory. My number is 555-7608. It'll be there. The directory probably has whoever's number this is."

I was actually starting to be afraid. I had the feeling that this cop would frame me if she could. She seemed desperate to believe I'd done something wrong. "Okay, do we have a directory here?" Principal Samson nodded yes. The cop asked everyone to leave the room before sitting down with me in private. "I don't know what kind of game you're playing but-"

"But I've been getting prank calls to my house nearly every day. You do nothing. I get beat up here every day - that's supposed to be illegal. And you do nothing. But the moment someone accuses ME of something, you'll do anything to make it true. You'll try to force me to lie and say I did it. When that doesn't work, you let one of my classmates hit me. I get it."

She got up and left. This cop already had it in for me. I needed someone here who was ON MY SIDE. Where were the Dagans?

She came back in with the school's directory. "I'm not going to do this for you. If you're insisting that it's someone else, then you find the number." She threw it on the table in front of me.

I was so angry that I was shaking. But I wasn't going to cry in front of these jerks. The Dagans were coming. I just had to hold out a little bit longer. I started at the back of the book and began to work my way forward.

I found it in 4 minutes flat. I could have probably guessed at it and found it in 4 seconds just by flipping to the one name I suspected over all the others: Jeremy Smith. The little round punk just couldn't leave me alone. I guess he didn't learn his lesson after the case of Alicia's missing sheet music. He was probably the same person who'd been calling my house at all hours of the night, making my parents wonder what "I'd done" to bring this on myself. I pointed it out to the cop. She asked if it was a friend of mine. I said no. She looked at me as if to call me a liar to my face and asked "Are you sure, cause if I ask him and it turns out-"

"Oh whatever. You've been trying to get me to lie all morning. Do you think I'm going to start now?" I thought she was going to hit me. But she just walked out of the room. I saw her show the name in the directory to Alicia and ask if it was one of my friends. Alicia's face turned completely dark when she saw the name. She knew exactly what had happened. She'd been played.

They pulled Jeremy out of class. He lasted 2 minutes in the conference room before he broke down crying like a little girl. He admitted to making the prank calls to Alicia's house, as well as about a dozen to mine.

The Dagans finally arrived, escorted by an FBI agent. After talking to me for a few minutes, the agent phoned the Plano Police Department's commanding officer and reamed him out over the phone. "Excellent police work. Just excellent. I haven't seen this top notch work since 'Keystone Kops'. You try to force a false confession out of a 12-year old kid, let another kid strike him while in custody, then you let him do all your investigating for you. What the hell kind of force are you running here, anyway?!?!?"

It did make me feel good to see the look on the cop's face when the Dagans arrived. I felt like "Yeah!!! The

Calvary has arrived!!! These are the guys in my corner - two Mossad agents, and the FBI - beat that!"

Mrs. Dagan looked like she was ready to kill everyone in the room for what they'd put me through. Like mother, like daughter, I guess.

None of the Peters family could even look me in the face. I was sent back to class without so much as an apology from anyone. But I didn't actually go to class. I walked out one of the doors behind the school when nobody was looking, and just sat on the concrete steps. It was a beautiful spring day, and I started to cry. I'd just been through hell, and nothing was going to change.

At that moment, I understood what drove the Dagans. I understood the Katzavs. I understood Mossad. I understood Israel. People hurt me today. And nobody would ever apologize. Nobody would ever lift a finger to make it right. Nobody had been interested in listening to me. Nobody had been interested in the truth. And this would not be the last time. I knew that much.

I also knew that I couldn't count on anyone to ever really stand up for me. The Dagans did today. And Zippy would probably walk into hell itself to protect me. But she couldn't be there all the time. I had to fend for myself.

I thought of the triumphant looks on the officers' faces when they put that machine down in front of me. I thought of the smile on Principal Samson's face when Alicia slapped me. I remembered the hate in her eyes. At that moment, the words flashed in my head "never forget."

And with that, I finally understood the Jewish mantra. I looked up to the sky, gritting my teeth. With burning anger welling up inside me, I imagined all the horrible and violent things I wanted to do to everyone who had hurt me. I tried to imagine all the terrible acts that would keep someone from ever hurting me again. In that moment, I growled out those two magic words, "NEVER AGAIN!!!!"

CHAPTER SEVEN – GUNS IN THE CLASSROOM

Saturday, April 28th 1990

I was absolutely giddy when I woke up this morning. Zippy had told me to clear out my entire schedule this afternoon for something "special." Since "normal" to her was off the scale awesome to me, I couldn't wait to see what she considered "special." Her parents came by right after lunch to pick me up.

We drove out to a closed building in a scary part of Dallas. I didn't realize where we were until Mr. Dagan unlocked the front door. I read the paper sign which was taped to it, "Gun Range Closed for Private Session." This had to be a joke. I walked inside.

"Have fun you two. Pick you up at 6:30." And with that, Mr. Dagan was off. We had this whole abandoned building to ourselves.

Zippy kissed her dad on the cheek, and then came running into the building with a huge backpack slung over her shoulder. She locked the door behind her, and turned to me, barely containing the overwhelming joy exploding inside her. "Today you learn to shoot gun!!!!!"

"I'm what?!?!? Why? I haven't even learned Krav yet. How-".

"You can no be effective at M-Gang unless you can carry gun, and you can no carry gun unless you can use it accurately. We going to do tactical firearm training with my parents pretty soon, and you need to be up to speed on handgun use before you can get any benefit from that lesson.

"So are the other M-Gangers joining us?" I was secretly hoping she'd tell me they weren't. I really liked the idea of a whole afternoon alone with Zippy.

"No."

Awesome.

"The other kids got started with their firearm training last September, so you a bit behind, but if I can to get you to where you can hit the target with at least some semblance of accuracy, you should be able to jump in. M-Gangers use Mossad's standard .22 Beretta. I use something considerably larger. I hope you will eventually use the same gun as me, but as long as I am your trainer, you're going to start with something in between."

She unzipped her backpack and rummaged through it for a few seconds. Then she pulled out a black cloth holster with a handgun in it. She took the gun out of the holster and showed it to me. I recognized it immediately from the James Bond movies. I couldn't help but point and say, "It's a Walther PPK." Then in my best faux-British accent, "seven six two millimeter, and stopping power like-"

"You watching too many movies. I chose Walther PPK because is concealable, no because of some Hollywood character. And until we get you a more permanent gun, is a good one to learn on. The worst thing in world that can happen for you right now is someone discover you carrying a gun. That would be very bad. But if this happens with a

PPK, you deserve for it to happen."

"Why not carry a Saturday Night Special then?"

"Are you kidding? Is a piece of JUNK. Those things just as likely to blow up in your hand as they are to kill the bad guy. I no thrilled about you carrying a PPK, but at least is more dangerous to bad guy than to you, unlike the Saturday Night Toy Pistol."

"Yeah, but the PPK's a really good gun, isn't it?"

"Um . . for training maybe. I can no think of any other use for it. Mossad agents carry these itty bitty Berettas. But I carry a much better gun."

She reached back into her backpack and pulled out this gigantic frightening black thing that looked like a cop's gun on steroids.

"This is Walther P88. It never jams, is the sturdiest handgun in existence, and best of all . . . I have SURGICAL accuracy at 75 feet with this gun. Only downside is a bit heavy, and is harder to conceal."

She handed it to me . . . and WHOA she wasn't kidding about heavy!! I gave it back to her and picked up the PPK she'd set out for me. I had to ask "Do all the kids in M-Gang train with something like that canon of yours?"

"No - just me, although I expect Sivan to get one any day now. She just HAS to compete with me."

"What do they train on?"

"The same Berettas they carry. These guns do no belong to the kids. They belong to Israeli government. They no just going to GIVE to you a $500 gun. Is issued to you, and you responsible for taking care of it and using it if you need to, but it remains the property of the government. The P88 is actually mine. I got issued a Beretta, but I prefer the 88. It was a birthday present last year. I test fired one at range with my dad, and just fell in love with it."

"So what's wrong with the James Bond gun?"

"Well, they jam a lot, so you never want to take it into firefight. Another problem is the PPK has dreadful accuracy. You never will be able to watch a James Bond movie again. I want you to learn with it because it's really easy to move from that to the Beretta. You just no want to shoot anything too far away."

"What do you do if there's a bad guy that far off, then?"

"Good question - even if you are getting a little bit ahead. The answer is that you should never use handgun for a target that far away. When the adrenaline is going, is just like a hand-to-hand encounter. You lose fine motor skills, so your accuracy sucks."

She took the gun from me, stood up, went over to the counter, and placed both guns side by side.

"Now, the first thing we have to cover is safety. There are only two safety rules for today. The first is that neither you nor I are ever in line of fire - ever! Rule number two is you never put your finger on trigger until you are ready to fire it."

She pulled a stack of papers with bulls-eye targets on them. There was a little string on the ceiling behind the counter. She clipped the piece of target paper onto the string and flipped a switch on the wall. The target slowly moved away from us 'till it was about ten feet away.

"Okay, now shooting is no just a matter of pointing the gun at the target and firing. Your whole body must be correct. Get into your fighting stance."

I jumped into a perfect Krav Maga stance right in front of the counter.

"Okay, now take the gun in your right hand without moving your feet or hips. Both feet pointing at target. Hips square with target. This is shooting stance as well as fighting stance. If your body is off, your aim will be off. Move your hand up the grip - it should be as high as possible on the grip. Hand high up on grip gives you better control over accuracy. Now point your finger forward down the barrel - you've got it!!!"

I sure didn't feel like I 'had it' by a long shot.

"Ok, watch." She picked up a magazine, slid it into her P88, pulled back on the rack, then placed it on the counter.

"Do the same with yours." I copied every motion. The slide was a lot harder to pull back than it looked, but I got it.

We both put our earplugs in and put these huge plastic eyeglasses over our faces, then she picked up the P88, and emptied the clip into the target. She turned and motioned for me to do the same. There were tons of holes right in the middle of the target. She wasn't kidding about surgical accuracy. I picked up the PPK, aimed right at the X, and BANG!!!!!!!

The gun nearly jumped completely out of my hands. I looked at the target . . . then back at Zippy . . . then back at the target . . . then back at Zippy. "Where's the hole?"

She came over and stood by my shoulder. "See the little hole in the bottom right hand corner of paper, about a foot and a half under the target?"

How the hell did that happen????????? I was aiming right at the center X. Apparently that was nowhere near good enough, and now Zippy was going to teach me how to shoot correctly.

My first mistake was holding the gun the way my dad had always told me - like you're holding a live animal: tight enough that it doesn't get away, but not so tight that you hurt it. According to Zippy "This is CRAP!!! It is no an animal. Is GUN. Crush the handgrip!!!!!"

My second mistake had been made with my eyes. I'd focused my eyes on the target . . to which Zippy asked "Why you still focusing on the target. You already decided it needs to be shot. Just aim to the center of it, let it become a blur and focus your eyes on the red dot at the end of your gun's barrel. The bullets will find their way to the right spot."

We went through ten magazines each, with her giving me lessons and pointers like these in between each magazine. Once we got my grip and my sighting worked out, all my bullets were going into the big circle. They just weren't all near the X yet.

We reloaded all ten clips at least five times - maybe more. We kept going 'till we ran out of boxes of bullets, and she'd packed a lot.

Mr. Dagan showed up just as we ran out of ammunition. He took us back to my place. Zippy stayed over while my parents, my aunt and uncle, and the Dagans all went to the Symphony. We ordered pizzas and watched TV all evening long. Elise dozed off during the Arsenio Hall Weekend Jam, which was great because I wanted to put on Fright Night, and Zippy didn't think it would be an appropriate movie for Elise. The adults all got home just after midnight. We all parted ways and I went off to bed.

My hands still hurt from all the shooting.

CHAPTER EIGHT – ZIPPY'S SOLUTION

My life followed a very simple pattern for the next three weeks. Either Sheri's dad or Rachael and Danny's mom would pick the three of us up from school and take us to M-Gang. Zippy, Sivan, Amir, and Aaron would usually already be there. We did firearm practice after school every Monday and Wednesday. We'd do Krav training every Tuesday and Thursday We'd also devote about one hour to homework each day. Our parents would come get us around 9 pm, get us a quick bite to eat, and we'd head home for bed.

Saturday and Sunday afternoons were also heavy on Krav Maga training.

And as suffocatingly planned out as that sounds, I remember it as the happiest time of that spring. Notice what I didn't mention, though? The 7 hours I was trapped at school. I had another routine there: one that involved figuring out which route from class to class would give me the most escape options if one of my classmates decided to beat me up. It also involved getting in and out of the boy's locker room as quickly as possible, changing clothes as close to the exit as I could.

Saturday, May 20th 1990

It was the last 2 day weekend of the year. Memorial Day was one week away, then there would only be four days of school after that. I was going to spend the entire day with Zippy. She would get home from her Synagogue around 1:30, then we'd go hang out at Collin Creek Mall for . . . well . . . the duration of the day.

However, things felt a little weird once we got there - like maybe we should have just stayed home and played board games or something. There were too many kids from school there. Zippy didn't seem to notice. She didn't have a care in the world.

Around six, we headed over to the food court. There was a Chick-Fil-A over in the corner, by the bathrooms and security office. We both ordered the chicken sandwich combo - and I finally took her advice to avoid the Coke, getting a lemonade instead.

I also finally mustered up the courage to ask her the question that had been lurking deep inside me for several weeks now. "Do you mind if I ask you something a bit more . . . personal than usual."

She smiled a bit. "You can ask anything. But I might hit you instead of giving you answer."

That wasn't exactly what I was hoping for, but this question had been gnawing at me, so here it went. "Is it true about you and the Iranian Special Forces team. The Sava-whatever-they're-called."

The smile instantly faded off her face. "Savak." Her face turned dark.

I tried to relax and ask as gently as I could. "Is that stuff really true?"

"Mark . . ." She paused for a minor eternity. "I do no talk about that with most people. You are very precious to me, so I will tell you this much. Yes, I kill entire team of

Savak. They were sent to kill my family. The USA did no protect us because their relationship with Israel had gone bad over Israeli spy getting arrested."

"Danny said something about that. He called it-"

"The Pollard incident. Yes. Many Israelis who work counter terror died because nobody protect their identities or locations, and Savak go on murder expedition."

"So what happened when they found you? Tell me about-"

"No!" She was getting upset with me. I could tell. "You looking for good action story. I no give you this. I kill four men. This all you need to know." She shrugged her shoulders, and went back to her sandwich.

I had to try and fix things. "I didn't mean to-"

"I know." She cut me off. "I just . . . tired of everyone make big deal about it."

We looked at each other for a few seconds before nodding and going back to our sandwiches. Then suddenly I heard a huge slurping noise behind me. I turned and saw the giggling faces of Chris Gomez, Dusty Adams, and Kevin . . I didn't know his last name. Chris was in my PE class, and came after me in the locker rooms several times. The other two were losers he hung out with.

He piped up for all the kids nearby to hear. "Hey, I've got $3.50. Anybody want a blowjob? Slurp, slurp."

They were doing this to me right in front of Zippy, who by now was slowly standing up - eyes fixed right on Chris. A small crowd of kids were starting to gather. I recognized most of their faces from my school, but I really didn't know any of their names. Dusty picked up where his buddy left off, "Fresh cock tastes good huh?"

"I know you." The look on Zippy's face said murder. She was ready to rip Chris's throat out. "You led the group of cowards who beat up a kid named Aaron Levin in your neighborhood last year." He looked at her like she was speaking a foreign language.

She continued, her body falling into that unnatural calm I saw back at the violin competition. "I give you one chance to apologize to Mark and leave. Then I hurt you . . . all of you." Holy crap!!! Was she threatening all three of them? I don't know if she realized this yet or not, but I wouldn't be much use in a fight.

"Check it out!!! Little faggot's got a bodyguard." Just as he said it, he must have noticed her Star of David necklace with the Hebrew writing on it. "And she's a Christ-Killer too."

They all three started laughing, then it dawned on him. "Oh, that little Jewish fudge-packer that lives on your street, Dusty. That must be the Aaron she's talking about. Yeah, that little faggot fought like a girl worse than Mark." They all laughed. "Don't you guys know that the Bible says you shouldn't suck dicks or kill Jesus?"

He'd sealed his fate. Zippy was going to hurt him VERY BADLY, even if it meant getting beaten down herself.

"What do you say we drag these two into the bathroom hall over there and have a little fun with them!!!" Kevin must have known what that threat sounded like when he said it, but I don't think he cared. The other two high-fived him. The crowd of kids around them was all giggling.

Zippy started walking directly towards Chris, then suddenly turned and shot one of her lighting fast MURDEROUS groin kicks right into Dusty. As soon as her foot hit the ground, she grabbed him by the hair and started viciously stabbing him in the face repeatedly with the little plastic knife from our dinner. I hadn't even realized she was holding a weapon.

She may or may not have been aiming at his eyes, but he screamed and puked at the same time. She must have stabbed his face at least five times before Kevin managed to rush over, grabbing her by the shoulders from behind. He'd fallen right into her trap. I knew every move she was going to make before she even did it.

Both of her hands shot up to her shoulders, plucking his hands off of her. She immediately slapped him in the groin, then her elbow shot up to catch his jaw just as his body was slumping from the groin slap. Pieces of his teeth went flying from his mouth. She spun around and palm-struck him in the face so hard that blood splattered everywhere. Nobody could react before she'd moved in, pulling his whole head into a clinch against her chest. BAM - she kneed him in the groin so hard his whole body came off the ground. At the exact moment his feet hit the ground - BAM, she'd kneed him again . . . just as hard. Chris tried to move in on her, but she spun Kevin around and used him as a human shield, keeping him in between the two of them. By now, he was puking his guts out down the front of her shirt.

BAM, BAM, BAM she kept kneeing him, and he kept puking. The other kids standing around all had horrified looks on their faces. BAM, his legs had completely buckled at this point, and Zippy was literally holding him up by his head just to keep kneeing him.

"Alright, he's had enough!!!" Chris wasn't laughing any more.

BAM.

"Come on!! He's had enough!!!" In fact, he was starting to sound desperate.

BAM.

"Please!!! Stop hitting him. He's REALLY hurt. Please!!!"

BAM.

"Stop it, for God's sake!!!!" She'd broken Chris without even touching him. He was begging, and on the verge of tears.

BAM BAM. I'm not sure how she was even holding Kevin up anymore. She grabbed the hair on the back of his head and - BAM - kneed him in the face. Blood splattered everywhere again. He slumped to the ground, and let out a sickening whining noise. It was like listening to something die. Chris just stood there with horrified shock on his face.

"What the hell, man! We were just messing with-"

"Yes, you were just MESSING with us . . just like you 'MESS' with Mark. You also just MESS with me. You also MESS with Aaron. It was all in good fun, no?"

She stepped a bit closer to him and said in a whisper, "Now I MESS with one or two of you. How you like it?" She looked around at the horrified looks on all the kids faces. "The next one of you to touch my boyfriend . . . "

Wait a minute . . did she just call me that?

". . . or call him a name, or whisper nonsense about bathrooms or blowjobs when he walk by, or the next of you to make obscene sounds when he walk by . . ." She pointed at the crying blobs on the floor. "I will do worse to either you or someone you love." The look on her face was absolute rage. I swear there was blood in the pupils of her eyes as she spoke. "Do you understand?" She was staring straight at Chris.

His face was still half in shock, but he managed to nod his head. She shot a quick glance around at the horrified crowd, and we left. We went to the record store on the other end of the mall and called Mrs. Dagan's car-phone. She picked us up at the exit on that end of the mall, and we headed out of there. We got home, and Zippy changed clothes - getting out of the smelly, vomit covered stuff she was in.

The police showed up at the Dagan house a few hours later. We gave them our side of what happened. It helped that one of the kids had called Zippy a "Christ-Killer," and that several of the witnesses had heard him say it. The witnesses had also heard him brag about beating up a Jewish kid in his neighborhood for no reason other than the kid's religion. Plano had a reputation for being "above" any racial or other forms of bigotry. The police wanted to keep it that way. The fact that they now saw the kids who came after us as motivated by hatred of Jews - that's something the police REALLY wanted to keep out of the papers.

It helped that Zippy had her "terrified little girl" act down to a science. She knew the exact words to use. "I was scared for my life. There were three of them. They said they were going to drag us over to the bathrooms and 'have fun with us.' I knew what he mean by that." She was crying by the end of her "interview" with the cop.

Wow, she was good!!!!

After they left, she called Aaron and told him all about it. She'd been waiting a long time to make that call. Aaron had been a friend long before she brought him into M-Gang. She'd wanted to do something about the thugs in his neighborhood for some time. It had taken a while, but she finally took care of the little punks for him. And she totally got away with it.

CHAPTER NINE – PLAYING WAR WITH REAL GUNS

Saturday, May 26th 1990

I woke up ridiculously early, but it was the perfect time to do it - Memorial Day Weekend. No school on Monday. Then there would only be three days of school left before summer would start.

The Dagans were scheduled to pick me up around 1 in the afternoon. We were doing a special 8-hour-a-day training this entire weekend. My parents were a bit annoyed because they wanted me to help out with this home improvement fiasco that my dad was attempting in the back yard.

I wanted nothing of it. They knew it. And that aggravated them to no end. But they were happy that I was at least doing something with the Dagans instead of just sitting around watching TV all day.

Like clockwork, the Dagans picked me up right after lunch. We headed off to a special outdoor training range used by the local police departments. All seven of my fellow M-Gangers were there, along with the Dagans and Mrs. Katzav. I now understood where Sivan got all her features. She was the young twin of her mother.

Mr. Dagan pulled me aside.

"Mark, how's your shooting?" He seemed so relaxed.

"Well, I'm always within the 8 ring at 20 feet, and I'm always within the nine at 10 feet."

He nodded in that typical Israeli way "Is good. Is good." He patted me on the back. "We issue you an official gun now. While other kids eat their lunches and adults setup the tactical range, why don't you go over to the basic range and get accustomed to it." He handed me a small black bag.

"Wow. Thank you."

"Don't thank me. Just get accustomed to it. The feel will be different than you're used to. You've got about a half hour. Put as many rounds through it as you can." He nodded again and was off. I went over to the shooting range counter. I got a feeling all the other kids were watching me, which I confirmed when I looked over at the picnic table where they were all eating. Yep. All eyes on Mark.

I opened the bag. There was a gun case inside, and three boxes of bullets. Inside the gun case was an itty-bitty Beretta. Zippy was right. The PPK was a cannon compared to this thing. I loaded up the magazine clips - Mr. Dagan had given me three, and they each held 8 rounds. I went through the exact same routine I'd gone through every couple of days for the last few weeks. After putting on the glasses and earmuffs, I got into my stance, aimed with a crush grip, took a breath, and squeezed . . . the gun didn't jump at all. It barely vibrated. I didn't even hear the pop. My first instinct was to look down the barrel of the gun to make sure it had gone off, but my internal safety alarm went off at the idea.

"You've gotta be kidding me." I'd said it by the time I

realized I was even talking. I looked, and it had barely made a little pinprick hole in the target, but it was RIGHT ON the X. I aimed again, and rapid fire emptied the clip - all on the X. This thing wasn't a gun. It was a toy. And I couldn't miss with it. I'd gone through all three boxes before I even realized it.

There was a quick tap on my shoulder - it was Zippy. "Can I have my Walther back now?" I laughed. What would I need the Walther for? I couldn't miss with this thing. Of course, I was still taking several seconds to sight in on the target, something I figured they'd be working out of my system today. I undid the holster from the back of my pants and handed it back to her. I looked in the bag - sure enough, Mr. Dagan had given me a holster to use with this Beretta. I clipped it to the back of my shorts, just like Zippy had taught me last month.

Mr. and Mrs. Dagan, along with Mrs. Katzav, had quite a lesson for us. First off, they gave us 40 boxes of ammunition each. FORTY BOXES!!!!! Then Mrs. Katzav taught us how to get into a shooting stance while pulling the weapon from the holster. We had to perform a specific series of motions, and we practiced them over and over. Mrs. Katzav kept shouting "Do not squeeze the trigger until you have sighted your target." We did it really slowly at first, then started picking up the pace.

Once we got good at it, Mr. Dagan took over and taught us how to shoot without sighting. That was scary, but it made perfect sense. You can point your finger at any target with pretty good accuracy, and your trigger finger is pointing at the target right up to the moment you put it ON the trigger. So you should be able to just point at the target and shoot.

During the last hour, we put it all together. We did the draw into our shooting stance, and fired without sighting. I could go from not having a gun in my hands to putting a bullet in the X with frightening speed. My muscles were getting so used to doing this that I could probably do it in my sleep. I guess this is how assassins are made.

Sunday, May 27th 1990

I really detested going to my parents' church. Every Sunday it was the same thing – standing, sitting, kneeling, bowing, and reciting stuff. And it wouldn't end. My parents wanted to stand around talking to everybody after the service was over. I felt trapped. I really hated it.

But once we got back home, the Dagans showed up. It was right back to the outdoor range with the gang. We had unfinished business.

Each of our ammunition stacks had been replenished to forty boxes per person. We spent the first hour practicing getting into our stance, drawing, and firing without sighting again. It felt off at first, but by the end of the hour, we were all doing it perfectly - just like yesterday afternoon.

We spent the next two hours going over some new concepts, like how to properly engage more than one person at a time and how to advance on an enemy during a firefight. It was mostly angles, proper speed, and ways to minimize danger to yourself.

We finished the day learning how to quickly clear a jammed gun so that we can get back to shooting, as well as shooting in weird positions, like kneeling, laying down, or even standing on a bouncy trampoline.

We stopped a little early so that we could all strip and clean our guns. Then we headed over to M-Gang Headquarters to get showers before heading home. No sense risking mom and dad noticing the gun-oil smell.

The Dagans dropped me off at Chili's. There I found my parents, aunt, uncle, Elise, and two of my parents' friends from church. They'd just ordered the chips and queso. I hadn't missed anything. So I joined in and told them all about my day at the . . . obstacle course, learning the value of teamwork and fair play. Yep. I was getting much better at lying.

Monday, May 28th 1990

Memorial Day - the last day of my mini-vacation before the final gauntlet that the next week would be. My hands were already sore when I woke up. I'd fired maybe 5,000 rounds through that little Beretta over the last two days, and I'd probably fire a few thousand more by the end of the day.

The Dagans showed up at about 9:30. We got to the range and practiced shooting under pressure. Mrs. Katzav was wearing boxing mitts. While we were shooting in either a standing or kneeling position, she'd walk by and start hitting us all over the chest, back, legs, and head with these mitts. And believe me, these weren't pats. She hit HARD.

The day ended with each of us running through an obstacle course where we had to put all our skills together. It was like playing war with real guns. I know it was a serious drill, but it was SO MUCH FUN that each of us wanted to do it again when it was over. Of course, everybody passed. How could we not? We were having the time of our lives out there. When it was all over, we spent our last hour cleaning the guns again. Then we headed back to M-Gang for showers to get the smell of gun-oil off of each of us.

I got back around six and had leftovers for dinner. I felt a twinge of sadness. I had a few hours left before bedtime, and then three more days of school. My mother took pleasure in pointing out "the holiday is over." If it hadn't been for the conversation I'd had with Zippy just before coming home, I might have been downright depressed. But all I had to do was survive three days. That's all I had to do.

Don't get knifed for three days. Don't get shot for three

days. Don't let gangs of kids beat you up for three days. Stay close to Danny and Sheri for three days.

CHAPTER TEN – STEEL WHEELCHAIRS

Wednesday, May 30th 1990

I didn't know it when I came home, but I'd just spent my last moments as a seventh grader. I got 12 major threats from fellow students. Each one promised that I was going to get beaten up or killed on the last day of school, since teachers could no longer really threaten students with detentions or anything. Sheri and Danny would only really be around for my first and fourth period classes, so I'd REALLY be on my own.

I spent the entire evening watching a Rolling Stones concert on TV. I'd never really listened to their music, but everyone called them the "greatest rock band" in the world, so I was curious. Besides, I had the night off from training. M-Gang was on hiatus all week to give us time to decompress and do our end-of-school stuff without distraction.

The show was awesome. I taped it, and I knew I'd be watching this tape again and again. Hell, I watched it again immediately after the broadcast was over.

Thursday May 31, 1990

To my utter shock, when I explained the death threats to my dad, he agreed to not make me go to school. I got to spend the entire day by myself. I watched my tape of the Stones concert . . twice. I also ran through the entire Krav Maga routine Zippy had taught me.

Sheri called Zippy the moment school was out to tell her I was missing, so she called me to make sure I was ok. Within the hour, every single kid in M-Gang had called to inform me of what a lucky kid I was to get to skip the last day of school.

I had three months of freedom. I also got another happy bit of news when my dad brought the mail in. My passport had arrived. I was going to Israel!!!!

June 1990

The entire month of June just blew by. My parents had been planning a road trip to Florida for months with my aunt and uncle. So I disappeared from M-Gang for a few weeks. Of course, the other kids were all doing their family vacations too, so I didn't really miss anything. Before leaving town, I made my way to a nearby record store to buy a copy of the new Stones album, "Steel Wheels." Like I said, the concert had been awesome.

We stopped for a day in Biloxi, Mississippi where I nearly got myself killed. I didn't know that people were still racists anywhere in America. I thought that was just stuff you read about in history books. So when we stopped at a hotel, I was really happy when a group of kids playing water-volleyball in the pool asked me to join. Of course I joined. It looked fun. It never occurred to me that everyone in the pool was black, and everyone sitting around the pool looking in was white.

It also never occurred to me that anyone would have a

problem with me playing with a group of kids who happened to be a different color than me. If Zippy had been here, she'd have scolded me for failing to be aware of my surroundings. As it was, every single person sitting around the pool was staring at me, and the looks on their faces were anything but friendly. I wonder if this was what it was like for Zippy and Sivan back in Israel.

From there, it was on to Orlando. I don't remember much about Disney World, other than hating it. It was hot, and there were thousands of people crammed into this concrete park that felt like an oven. We stood in line for hours to go on 5 minute rides that bored the crap out of me. The only ride I enjoyed was an indoor roller-coaster which had a ridiculous name like "Space Thunder" or something. Like I said, it was forgettable.

I tried to take note of everything, because Zippy had told me that a trip to Disney World would make for a much better cover story than anything we could ever make up when our classmates ask us what we did this summer. Since I wouldn't be able to tell anyone outside of my family about my impending work in Israel, I'd need a cover story. So my cover was going to be me doing a lot of talking about my week at Disney - so much that nobody would ever wonder what I did the rest of the time.

But honestly, the three days we spent there were so mind-numbingly boring that I found myself trying to FORGET details.

Our return drive took us back to small-town Mississippi, where I was careful to avoid any pools. This vacation just plain sucked. I couldn't wait to get back to sparring and shooting with my friends at M-Gang.

The whole time we were in the car, my uncle kept cracking jokes about me liking the new Stones album so much. He called it "Steel Wheelchairs" in reference to their age. He didn't think that people their age should still be doing rock shows.

When we got back, Zippy quizzed me on all the details of my vacation. She insisted on me committing these to memory and pretending that it was much cooler than it actually was. I understood why, but I didn't think she really appreciated how boring the whole thing was. Maybe I wasn't communicating it right, because she seemed way too interested in every last word. The last two weeks of my life didn't really deserve that much interest.

It was the next couple of weeks where things were supposed to get interesting.

CHAPTER ELEVEN – USELESS IDIOTS

Monday, July 9th, 1990

The excitement among the M-Gangers was electric. We were only two days away from our big trip to Israel. Everyone's passports had come in. Everyone's visas were ready. But I don't think anyone had packed one single item of clothing.

Of course, I'd need to pack while my parents weren't looking. Seeing me pack a .22 handgun with four magazines and 6 tactical folding knives really wouldn't go over well. Mr. and Mrs. Dagan always promised to take care of the situation if my parents ever found out, but largely put the onus on me to keep my parents in the dark. That meant good grades, no displays of anger while at home, and polite conversation about any topic they'd find boring, like the detailed history of one of my favorite bands. That would have them rolling their eyes in a heartbeat.

Speaking of my favorite bands, I heard an advertisement on the radio saying that one of my favorite bands was coming to Dallas: The Moody Blues. Yep, the MTV synth-pop band that did that tune on the Karate Kid movie. I hadn't listened to their stuff much over the last year, but I had dusted off some of their tapes this past couple of weeks, and packed them along with my new Stones tape for the plane ride, along with a couple of extra sets of batteries for my Walkman. I might not have one item of clothing packed, but I've got my tapes. A guy's gotta have his priorities.

Tuesday, July 10th, 1990

The last day before the big trip. I spent the day going from store to store with my mom, who seemed intent on buying me much more stuff to take to Israel than I could ever hope to pack.

We all had dinner together at home. My mom cooked angel hair pasta with pesto, a favorite of mine. I usually tried to avoid spending so much time with my family, but tonight it just seemed right. They were worried about what may happen while I was in Israel. I was just worried about getting through the flight. I'd never been on a plane ride that had lasted for more than an hour before. Now I was going to be on one for more than 12 hours non-stop. That was so going to suck.

But tonight was a family night. And I loved my family. I just couldn't stand them half the time . . . still loved them though.

Wednesday, July 11, 1990

Flying off to a foreign country can be exciting, until the day of the trip. Then it's scary. All these things go through your mind. The first thoughts are of your own mortality. The plane might crash. Will it hurt? Is there really a heaven? What happens to all my memories when there's no more me? Yes, you can torture yourself for a while with those thoughts.

And when I'm done tormenting myself over my impending doom, then I start worrying about other things. What if their customs people don't let me in? What if I can't get back home. What if there's a terrorist attack and I get killed over there? Oops. We're back to that impending doom thing. Did I mention how good I am at torturing myself?

When we got through security at the airport, all the M-Gangers were high-fives and hugs. Nobody had gotten stupid and tried to walk through the metal detectors with a gun. Those were all packed into something called the "diplomatic bag" which nobody was allowed to look into except Israeli personnel.

My parents were being unusually clingy with me. My mom seemed terrified to let me go on this trip, but my dad was insistent. They were both, however, absolutely positive that I was going to call them in under a week, begging to come home. They didn't think I could handle being in a foreign country.

This was also a great "getting to know you" session for all the M-Gang parents. Everybody knew the Dagans, but nobody seemed to know each other, so it was great to see my parents, the Azels (Sheri's Parents), the Steins (Rachael and Danny's parents), the Levins (Aaron's parents), and Mrs. Katzav all getting along.

Most of the people in the waiting area were Jewish, and there was group of older couples "making Ayliah" which is sort of a combination of a religious experience with immigrating to Israel. Everything was fine until this couple walked in who looked like my mom's derelict friends from high-school. These two just screamed "college campus protesters who never grew up and are still stuck in the 60s." Worst of all, they were wearing T-Shirts that said "Amnesty International" on them.

All of the people in the terminal seemed to look at them with absolute disgust.

"Oh great." Mrs. Dagan muttered. "The useless idiots are here."

I heard her say it as she walked by. My parents were busy talking to the Azels, so I took Elise by the hand and walked over to ask her what she meant.

"They're part of a 'Free Palestine' protest that a bunch of idiots from all over the world are going to be doing in Jerusalem next week." She paused for a few seconds and muttered again "Best justification I've ever heard for the invention of the Uzi."

I didn't understand. "Why would they do that? Don't Israelis try to help the Palestinians living in Israel?"

She smiled. It seemed no matter how stupid a question I could ask, she always took pleasure in educating me on things others would just assume I should know. "Yes, but you can't tell western idiots that. They're too in love with the terrorists who try to kill Israelis in the name of the Palestinian people."

Her voice started to get louder, "These people have their heads so full of idealistic notions about revolutions and such. They're usually college students, or adults who never outgrew their college days. They idolize monsters. The monsters usually refer to these people as 'useful idiots' but to the rest of us, they're not much use at all."

I still didn't quite understand, "But when people see things like mass murders done by terrorists, why do they still want to like them?"

"Do you think the whole world supported Hitler when he started murdering our people?"

I shrugged my shoulders.

She continued, "They did. He was loved on college campuses before World War II started. If there's one thing academic socialists have always been willfully blind to, it's Jewish suffering. It's no different now. They lie about Israel. They say we're no different than South Africa with the apartheid thing. They say we are the persecutors and oppressors. They say that the murders and terrorists are "resistance" and that our people are racist and oppressive. The lies change. But the anti-Semitism behind the lies remains."

Sivan's mom had come over to see what was getting Mrs. Dagan so worked up. She patted Mrs. Dagan on the shoulder and continued, "Mark, you must understand that we Israelis want to coexist with the Palestinians. And we did so rather well until other Arab nations started meddling and stirring up trouble between us and the Palestinians. Now we have to fear our own neighbors because of what these outsiders have stirred up."

She looked at the two idiots and continued, "And these American troublemakers are no different." She smiled and looked back at me, "Nobody wants to help the Palestinians more than we do. In fact, my late husband Shlomo spent much of his time in the IDF doing humanitarian work among non-combatant Palestinians. He even worked to get the Israeli government to use his humanitarian work as a template for other IDF units. We have no hatred for Palestinians. We want them to do well. We just refuse to die for them."

She looked at the couple with absolute disgust in her eyes. "But these people merely use phony concern for Palestinians as a pretext for their own anti-Semitism. When Americans and Europeans use the words 'Free Palestine,' they really just mean to say 'Heil Hitler.' Never forget that, Mark." With that, she headed off to the bathroom.

The time finally came for us to board. I hugged Elise and my parents goodbye. They were barely able to hold back the tears.

We boarded. The plane was only about half full by the time they closed the doors. I had a window seat with NOBODY booked in the two seats next to me.

That's right. I had an entire row to myself - not that it mattered much once the plane got in the air. Everyone seemed to just get up, walk around, congregate in various corners, and ignore the flight crew altogether. Zippy and Sivan managed to organize a big poker match with several M-Gangers (myself included) and a couple of the tourists.

About the only people we all ignored were the two idiots from Amnesty International. They were wise to sit in their chairs and do their best to remain invisible.

The poker game took a few hours, but Zippy collected quite a bit of money from everyone else by the time it was over.

Nighttime came and went very quickly, which is true anytime you fly from the US to a foreign country across the Atlantic. But nobody was interested in sleeping. The M-Gangers were all practicing telling our cover stories to adults on the plane. I explained to many old people that I was part of a religious group going to work at a Kibbutz farm (Kibbutz farms are charity farms in Israel where people work for free just to do a good deed). They all thought it was great that kids in the US were so close to their Israeli roots. Little did they know.

I also lost myself into my Walkman for a few hours. I had my new Rolling Stones tape. I listened to it while staring out the window, just like I had during my family's road trip to Disney last month. It was a great tape for long trips. I loved it.

But I didn't love the absolute garbage that passed for food on this flight. Thank God I packed a can of Pringles, or I might have otherwise starved. The food was awful. Even Zippy, who'll try anything, looked like she'd puke from the smell alone. She promised me that there'd be good food once we got to our dormitory outside of the Wingate Training and Fitness facility in Tel Aviv, where we'd spend the majority of our time.

That was good to know. I was dying for something to eat. But when we landed, I found that there was something other than food to worry about – the weather. Anyone who's ever been to Israel could tell you how HOT it is. Being from Texas, I thought I was ready for it.

I was dead wrong!!!

The moment they opened the door it was like someone blew Hell's own hairdryer into the plane. I was sweating like crazy before even getting to the door. Then I stepped out into the hot sun. Texas had nothing on this place. I swear I must have gotten a sunburn walking from the plane to the terminal entrance. Mr. Dagan was the first to go through customs and security. He explained to the officer who he was and who the M-Gang children were. Then they sped all 8 of us through, with Mrs. Dagan and Avi coming in behind us. Sivan's mom was off elsewhere doing . . . who knows what. I did get a good look as the Amnesty International couple was whisked off to a private room. I had a feeling that they were going to have a rough day.

They piled us all into a van, then took us out to the suicidal maze of raceways that comprise the streets of Tel Aviv. Everyone drives their cars at the maximum speed, regardless of how many cars are on the road, how many lanes there are, or whether there are turns. They don't even slow down for 90 degree turns. They just go all out all the time. Of all the adventures we had in Tel Aviv, I think one of the scariest was our drive from the Airport to our dormitory - a place which we quickly renamed "M-Gang Israel" or "M-Gang Headquarters Israel."

There were two kids to each dorm room. I was with Danny. Zippy and Sivan shared a room, which made sense. Let the two Israeli girls room together. That way neither has to worry about speaking English. It kinda backfired as they became more like sisters than anything we'd seen before. They spent so much time together that the rest of us started calling them the "Sabra Sisters." Sabra is a Hebrew word which we all learned very quickly. It means someone who's actually born in Israel.

As for the rest of the kids, Rachael and Sheri were

together, and Aaron and Amir were together. The Dagan parents got a family room with Avi. Mrs. Katzav was staying with her sister in town.

We all got supper in a little cafeteria which seemed to be there just for us, then headed back to the dorm's lounge room to hang out for a while. We were all pretty wiped out from the flight, but we wanted to see what there was for us in the lounge. We had a TV, VCR, pool table, ping-pong table, and a few couches. They didn't have many movies for us to watch, but the ones they had were all pretty cool.

This was looking to be a good summer.

CHAPTER TWELVE – WELCOME TO SHABAK

Thursday, July 12, 1990

We all woke up late - around 9:00 in the morning. We had wanted to go work out, but WOW is it hot in Israel. Did I mention that already? That and we didn't have time. We were due to meet our control officer in Israel. Zippy knew her already, and had assured us all that "Sarah is awesome - you will love her." We were also supposed to meet someone named Rebecca from Mossad. Zippy sort of knew her as well, but didn't seem to think we'd have much to do with her. She was the first official person we met, though. It was right after breakfast. She just sort of nonchalantly walked into our training room.

"Shalom, everyone. I'm Rebecca Pardo. I'm the case officer officially responsible for MYOP activities worldwide. The Dagans are operationally in charge in America, but as the program takes off, I'll be coordinating all youth agents worldwide from my office here. I will also follow your development very closely."

She paused, "This is important because typically our agents can only be in the field for a VERY limited time period, like a year or less, before we pull them out for life."

That part seemed confusing. We were all thinking the same thing. Rachael spoke up. "But why? After all the time spent training us, why wouldn't an agent be in the field for decades???"

"Fieldwork is a dark thing. It's dangerous and often times extremely violent. Even when it's not, you're lying all the time and living a fake life. It messes with your head to live in that world, and we've found that when we let people stay in the field for too long, they become mentally unbalanced, and sometimes they become a danger to everyone around them. We're not in the business of creating monsters. We've got enough of those trying to kill us without training our best and brightest in how to kill, and then turning THEM into monsters."

I think we were all feeling a little sick over this. We'd all be finished in less than a year? That completely sucks. This time I spoke up. "Wait a minute. Can't an agent ever be in the field longer than that? I mean, we're all . . . " I couldn't finish the sentence.

"The longest I've ever let someone work as an agent is 2 years. But you kids will be an interesting story. You guys are the test case for this new program. In fact, we had no idea there'd be so many of you. We were expecting to recruit four at the most, and have that whittled down to 2 by the time you came over here for a visit."

Aaron's hand went up. "So are we going to be doing fieldwork now?"

"No. You kids can't simply move into fieldwork. We train for three years. You've trained for 8 months, and all of your training has been in hand-to-hand and weapons combat. This is valuable, but you need to also train in navigation, secret communications, how to avoid getting on the radar of counter-intelligence, how to avoid being watched either by car or foot, and how to avoid getting set-up or captured. These are the true parts of trade-craft, and it's what we spend most of our training time on. Very few of our agents ever spend as much time on hand-to-hand combat as you kids have. And you've barely even started on any of the other skills."

There was an incredible sinking feeling that passed through the entire room. We all thought we were ready, and she was telling us that we'd barely even begun to train.

"We also require our agents to work a number of support missions before going live. If any of you kids end up serving with us . . . and I'm sure Tsipporah here will . . . you will excel at your job, because you're going to be performing support missions this summer with your field handler, my friend Sarah, who's running a bit late this morning." She looked at her watch. "I've actually got to go now, but she should be along any minute. Shalom." She pulled Zippy aside and had a quick QUIET conversation with her in the corner. Zippy kept looking back at me while they were whispering, then Rebecca left.

After she left, Zippy seemed annoyed. She grabbed Sivan, and the two went off to a corner to talk. They were whispering . . . okay, HISSING at each other in Hebrew. Something Rebecca had said clearly had Zippy upset with Sivan. It was getting worse by the second. They seemed like they were just about to come to blows when the door opened and this girl popped her head in.

She was mid-twenties, and possibly the most beautiful creature I'd ever laid eyes on. I was star-struck in love at first sight with this lady. How did something this gorgeous exist on this planet? My inner jaw was dropped to the floor. She had ash blonde hair pulled back in a pony-tail, and eyes that literally glowed. She was wearing army pants, army boots, and a loose white T-shirt. Zippy ran over to her. They hugged, and kissed each other's cheeks. Then she looked at the rest of us.

"I'm Officer Sarah Rabin. You can call me Sarah. I do not work for Mossad. I work for Sherut ha-Bitakhon ha-Klali . . you can call it Shabak for short. We're known in the US and Europe as Shin Bet. But if you call us by that name, we know you're not one of us. And whatever you do, DO NOT confuse Shabak with Savak. Savak are very bad guys from Iran. Shabak are good guys in Israel."

A couple of the girls chuckled, but the rest of us were clearly lost. Weren't we here to work for Mossad? What the hell is Shabak? Maybe she saw the confusion on our faces.

"The main difference between us and Mossad is that they work outside of Israel, while we work inside. So while you kids are in the US, they're in charge of you. While you're here in Israel, you're our problem. Specifically, you're MY problem. I will coordinate your training, your mission planning, and I will oversee your field operations. But I'm not your mom or your babysitter. We expect you kids to take care of yourselves for the most part. If you can't handle it, go home. Any questions?"

The room was dead silent.

"Good. We did a test run of this program last year with Ms. Dagan. She did four missions with us last summer, and was seen near so many Shabak raids that some local Palestinian groups started telling stories of the 'Angel of Death' - a child who was a bad omen of an impending raid where terrorists would get killed. This 'angel's' description sounded remarkably like you, Tsipporah." Zippy smirked a bit when she said it.

"So this summer, we plan to build on this "Angel of Death" legend."

"Yeah." The Sabra Sisters high-five'd each other. The whole room seemed to breathe a sigh of relief. They actually DID want to use us. We weren't just going to be training like Rebecca had suggested.

"We may even make a few more death angels while

we're here." The whole room was smiling at this point.

"Does anyone here have any experience outside of training - like being in a real fight?" Everyone looked at Zippy.

"Oh yes, I've been waiting nearly a year to ask you about this, Tsipporah. After you went back to USA last summer, someone told me this little tale about you taking out an entire Savak wet team by yourself. This is true?"

Zippy looked at the floor. She seemed a mix of embarrassment and sadness as she shook her head and whispered "Yes." If I didn't know better, I'd think she was trying to keep herself from crying. This was totally wrong. Zippy looked . . . vulnerable . . . fragile even.

Sarah on the other hand looked absolutely amazed. "Why didn't you tell me this last year? I thought we had no secrets?" Zippy whispered something in Hebrew that I couldn't understand, and Sarah responded "How many were there?"

Zippy choked a bit, "Arba." I knew that word. It meant "four."

"And how old were you when you do this?"

"Tishah." That meant nine.

Sarah just stood there stunned. "Wow. Angel of Death indeed." Zippy was still looking at the ground, which Sarah was going to have none of. "Look at me Tsipporah. You did an amazing thing, and you are an amazing girl. Never let anyone tell you otherwise. There's no telling how many innocent lives you saved."

Sivan put her arms around Zippy and hugged her. It was an oddly out of place tender moment. It only lasted for a few seconds before Sarah broke it with some levity. "So Tsippi," I was REALLY going to have to get used to people calling her by her Hebrew name. I'd gotten SO used to Zippy. It just seemed wrong. "It's been a year. Do I finally get to know what the "L" in your name stands for this summer?"

Everyone in the room gasped. We all knew better than to ask THAT question. I knew her name cause I'd heard her parents call her by her full name just once. Nobody else knew. She just stared at Sarah for a few moments, and responded. "That's MY SECRET. I do have a secret, you know."

Sarah's face lit up. Somehow Zippy had just told her what her middle name was without anybody nearby catching on. Sarah nodded, and let it go. A few seconds later, and she was back to being our handler instead of Zippy's old friend.

"Ok, we need to prepare you guys for your first live missions. First, let me explain how this works - forget whatever you've heard about the Mossad super-agent. I'm a Shabak agent. I know many Mossad agents. We're not super-heroes. We're not indestructible. And we're not these unstoppable dealers of death. What we are is a TEAM. You've heard the saying 'no man is an island.' We live this. You are never sent on a mission alone. There are always at least four people on a team with designated roles. These positions are named after the first four letters in the Hebrew alphabet: Aleph, Beit, Het and Ayin."

"The Aleph actually captures or kills the target, depending on the mission. This person does nothing else. It is the responsibility of the rest of the team to make sure that Aleph only has to do is show up, kill or capture, and leave."

"The Beit guards the Aleph. The Beit clears the way for the Aleph, creates distractions so that the target doesn't realize the Aleph is coming, and stops anyone or anything which might otherwise interact with the Aleph."

"The Het creates the covers for the Aleph and Beit. The Het is also responsible for mission planning, and making sure everyone knows their codes, covers, and stuff like that."

"The Ayin is responsible for watching the target up to

the point where the Alephs and Beits take over, then this person is responsible for escape routes and getting everyone out, once the mission is accomplished."

"You kids are going to be Beits, Hets, and Ayins on the missions we have prepared for you this summer. You will not be Alephs - that will usually fall to the special forces guys in Sayeret Matkal." I'd heard Zippy use those two words before. That's what they called the most elite guys in the Israeli Special Forces. Those guys were scary good. "They are the Alephs because they do killing and capturing better than anyone."

With that there was a lot of moaning from our group. We were all a bit disappointed that we'd come this far only to watch someone else get into the real action.

"Knock it off. We don't believe in everyone doing everything. The special forces guys do capturing and killing best. Let them do that part. You will best serve in the support roles, and that's what you kids are here for - to serve!!! Besides, with all the action you'll be seeing, I can't imagine any of you will want the Aleph spot when it's all over."

A dozen sighs of resignation later, and we all watched her thumb through a few files before looking at Zippy.

"Tsipporah, you're in charge of this group while I'm gone. Lunch is at 11:30. Just show up in the mess hall. They've been warned to expect you. We will begin navigation, mission study, and mission specific training this afternoon. And you will do your Krav Maga training in the evenings."

"You will no be joining us for Krav?" Zippy sounded devastated.

Sarah laughed. "You are a formidable sparring partner, Tsippi. I think I let you train with your friends. Besides, having my ass handed to me by a 13-year old will be too much devastation for my fragile ego this year. Krav for you will be all about teaching your friends. If you want to train for yourself, I'll arrange with the Special Forces guys to get you into the Matkal Krav sessions."

Sarah looked around and caught the eager looks on Sivan and Amir's faces. "Just Dagan. The rest of you train under her." They both huffed. She looked back at Zippy. "Please leave the IDF with a FEW of our Special Forces soldiers intact. Try not to put them all in the emergency room."

"I'll see what I can do."

Sarah started to leave the room. "Oh, one more thing. You're not prisoners here. You are free to come and go as long as you make all your trainings and required mission meetings. But be warned, most of your parents think you're here doing work at the Kibbutz farms, and if any of you get into trouble while you're off site, that's exactly where you'll spend the rest of your time in Israel. Also, there is a chance some of you may be onsite during an actual terrorist attack. If this happens, beware of anyone after the attack who behaves too calmly. That's the first indication that this is a terrorist who intends to continue the attack. Also know that in this situation, the guys with the black cards are in charge. They're special military guys trained in first response counter terror work. They outrank police - they even outrank us in those situations. Follow their orders to the letter."

She opened the door, turned back towards us once more, and with the most dead-pan bored voice imaginable, said "Welcome to Shabak."

After she was gone, Zippy turned to the crowd of us with the biggest beaming smile ever. "Isn't she awesome?!?!?!?!?!."

Everyone was nods and shrugs, so I volunteered "She's cool."

"You think she's hot, admit it." Zippy always saw right through me. Normally I'd be embarrassed at this question. But I never felt embarrassed around this crowd. I freely admitted it. And nobody gave me TOO much trouble over it. Sivan snorted and gave Zippy a condescending look.

She shrugged it off, rounded everybody up, and led us to our first class - Navigation 101. It was a huge room with overhead projectors aiming at every wall, and a map in the center of the room. Our first navigation test was going to be in a week, and we had to pass to move on to doing mission support.

Zippy explained that the test would be easy. We'd be blindfolded, and taken to a random spot in the city, where we'd be dropped off with nothing but a map, an ID, and enough money for a pay-phone call. We'd have one hour to make our way to a particular meet-up point. "Make it in time, and you pass. Get there late, or give up and call to be picked up and I shoot you myself." So we practiced and practiced. How do you figure out where you are just by landmarks? It's easy when you're looking at a map from the birds-eye view. It's a lot harder when you aren't quite sure where on that map you are. I think I was more nervous about this than I was the other parts of our training.

Zippy agreed that we'd all help each other by doing little mini tests when we were out on break, visiting the mall or going to various hangouts in Tel Aviv. We'd get a map, find a spot on it, and say "go there" without pointing out where we are to each other. There'd be no time limit. We'd just see if the M-Ganger chosen for the mini-test would be able to do it. It was a game, and we were all good at it. We all enjoyed it, and it guaranteed that none of us would be too nervous during our test.

Krav training, however, was WAY more intense!!!!! We began working on "third-party protection" - which means what to do when someone is pointing a gun at your friend. Zippy made us verbally say what we were doing as we did it. It was weird, but I got used to reciting over and over: "burst forward, open close, right hand on the trigger guard, left on his forearm, both thumbs to the sky, push pull, side head-butt, break and take." You always end up breaking the bad-guy's hand, and taking the gun away from him. Once you have the gun, back away while racking the gun's slide (to clear any jams) and tapping the magazine (to make sure it's still got bullets).

We spent the rest of our Krav training time sparring. We'd all put on these head-shields, boxing gloves, and shin pads . . and go at each other full force. Nothing was off limits but shots to the throat, cause those would be fatal. Everything else was fair game. We'd go for two minutes, then we'd rotate partners.

I got my butt kicked a lot. I had this bad habit of backing up and trying to get away from punches and kicks. Zippy kept telling me "Stay in fight!!! No take yourself out of fight. You MUST to stay in!!!!" But when those bright blue gloves were coming in at my face, and all I saw was a nonstop barrage of incoming blue, it wasn't easy to move forward. And when I would move forward, a kick would usually come in, either to my stomach, ribs, or groin (and the cup was only providing so much protection). So I really sucked at this free-style fighting thing.

Finally, Zippy decided she'd had enough. She made me stand still while she'd punch me in the face with her boxing gloves on. She'd hit me once (not too hard) and say "Did that hurt?"

"Not really."

BAM. "Did THAT hurt?"

"Not really."

BAM "Did THAT hurt?"

Ok, that last one did rattle my head a bit. "Not too bad."

"Stop being afraid!!! Move forward."

Whenever she'd spar with me, Zippy would go slowly and instruct me on combinations to move in on her with. Then we'd pick up the speed a bit. She never really pummeled me. But Amir, Sivan, and Aaron did. The boys would come in with a barrage of fists and pin me against a wall. Sivan would always lock up on me and drill me with knee shots to my mid-section till I'd crumple. The rest of the kids went easy on me and tried to make me a better free-style fighter.

It wasn't long before I was able to hold my own against all of the kids in the group except Zippy and Sivan. I could always count on Zippy to bring her fighting down to my level, and not just blast me. Sivan, on the other hand, would just do her level best to send me to the hospital.

True to her word, Sarah arranged for Zippy to train with the Special Forces guys. She came back to the dorm one night with some rather scary bruises on her arms and lower ribs - which she proudly showed off to every one of us. But she was thrilled with herself. She'd held her own against some of the greatest fighters in the world. She had every right to hold her head up high. She'd earned it.

CHAPTER THIRTEEN – HIT THE GROUND SKIPPING

July 13-20, 1990

Oddly enough, the first week at M-Gang Israel was more of a vacation than anything resembling work. The people in charge seemed to have the idea that we had to have some special "fun" experiences planned for us like we were on a cruise or something, so two major "fun" events were planned for our first week.

We all became intimately familiar with two locations in Tel Aviv - Dizengoff Street and Dizengoff Mall. Everything you could ever want to see, buy, or do was on Dizengoff Street. You could spend an entire summer just on that one street and still not see it all. Dizengoff Mall was the most awesome place on the planet. Then there were our accommodations. Just outside of our little dormitory, we had a pool!!!! What could be better?

Right in the middle of our first week, we spent about three days learning how to ride motorcycles. That was insane, especially TURNING. You have to lean into a turn, which feels scary because the bike is already leaning as you turn. You feel like you're going to go splat, but you don't.

We all woke up with heat exhaustion symptoms the next day, and ended up spending a day in bed, right in the middle of our "vacation" week. But after that, we were quickly back to our routine of hanging out at Dizengoff, or by the pool outside our dormitory.

The last day of our "off" week came much too quickly, A few of the kids were eager to get into real missions. But I could have used a few more days of fun in Tel Aviv. We headed down to breakfast as usual, but the day quickly took a weird turn.

The Sabra Sisters walked in giggling and smiling like they knew something we didn't. Zippy poured an orange juice for each of us, and Sivan collected everybody's plates off the table. Amir protested, but Sivan smacked him, and that brought an end to that. Zippy picked up her glass, enjoying the undivided attention of everyone at the table. "I would not be eating such big breakfast if I were any of you."

We all thought she was crazy. The way we'd been working out during our training time, we'd all pass out if we tried going on an empty stomach.

Sivan was actually smiling. This could be a very bad thing. She gave us a small hint. "Krav is cancelled for the day. So is shooting range. We'll be doing something else." She could barely contain herself. Both the Sabras burst out laughing again. Just then, Sarah walked into the room wearing a ridiculously poofy suit. "Everybody get into comfortable clothes, get your sunglasses, and meet me in front of the van in 15 minutes."

We all bolted. Whatever it was, anything that could make Sivan Katzav giggle was worth the price of admission. The van took us through the streets of Tel Aviv. I don't know what it says about me that these streets which terrified me only days ago now seemed normal.

We ended up on a military base outside of town, driving through several layers of tight security, and having our credentials checked, rechecked, and rechecked again. Finally, we all got out of the van in the middle of an airplane hangar. There, Sarah slowly got out, put on her sunglasses, and said "We thought you should all get a special treat before you go live, so we've arranged with the IAF to let each one of you have a turn flying an F15."

Stunned silence!!!!!!!

"Well, don't everybody get all excited and ask to be the first one up."

More stunned silence!!!!! I couldn't believe the words that had just hit my ears. I was going to get to fly a military fighter jet - a REAL military fighter jet. Those had to be the coolest words to ever drift through the air.

"Well, if nobody wants to volunteer, I guess we can just go back to M-Gang and do fighting drills."

Somehow, we all forced ourselves to snap out of the shock. We were all bursting with excitement. No wonder the Sabras were so giggly at breakfast!!! Then it occurred to me - no wonder they told us not to eat. Who wants to clean vomit out of a cockpit?

Since we had absolutely no training in avionics, take-off, landing, or anything having to do with navigating the panels of buttons, switches, blinking lights, and screens that make up the F-15's dashboard, we were all going to be riding in a 2-man trainer version of the plane. The pilots were going to take off, show us how to do some basic moves, let us do some basic moves, let us take over for about 15 minutes each, then give us a "thrill ride" pulling off some more impressive . . . er . . . make you sick as hell and nearly black-out . . . moves. It was AWESOME!!!!!!!

The planes you fly in when you go from city to city have NOTHING on these things! You feel EVERYTHING. Every bump, every turn, every micro-move the pilot makes goes rushing through your entire body.

When it was my turn, I was REALLY scared the first time I grabbed the throttle. The pilot was a nice guy named Benjamin, who insisted on calling me "Texas" for the entire flight. He showed me how to turn right, turn left, go up, go down, and roll. Then he showed me how to control the speed. Then after giving me some additional ground rules (additional to the "your pilot is a deity and you obey his commands like they were scripture" rules we got from Sarah before taking off) he let me fly!!!!

This was possibly the greatest day of my life. We rolled, we sped over the desert, we climbed to the sky like Chuck Yeager at the end of "The Right Stuff." The part where I was in control was over almost as quickly as it started. Then Benjamin gave me the thrill ride of my existence. At one point, the whole world started turning reddish, and I couldn't see anything. The next thing I knew, my head hit the headrest behind me. I could hear Benjamin chuckling over my headset, "you started to black out, Texas." I'd never been knocked unconscious before, so I didn't realize what was happening till it had already happened.

After my flight was over and the world stopped spinning, those of us who'd been up in the air stood around comparing notes. Those who hadn't been up yet stayed on the other side of the hangar, not wanting to spoil the experience.

We all got back to M-Gang, still shaking from the day's excitement. That's when Sarah hit us with the bad news. "This day is a test. The single hardest part of being an agent is that you will do amazing things. You will do things which are exciting beyond anything an ordinary person ever experiences. You will do things that affect the entire world and affect history itself. AND YOU CAN NEVER TELL ANYONE. This is the hardest part - being so excited, but convincing those closest to you and those you love that you've just had another boring day."

She paused for a moment to let that all sink in.

"Tonight, each of you who are not Sabras will call home. Your test is to never let them know what happened here today. You cannot utter one word about today's events. The only thing that happened today is that you all engaged each other in a football . . or what you Americans call SOCCER match. You can make it as exciting as you want, but this is all that happened today. One breath about flying, and you will have failed yourself out of the Mossad Youth Outreach Program."

Wow!!! If they wanted to test our ability to keep things from Mom and Dad, they certainly figured it out a way to take that test to the hilt. What kid in his right mind wouldn't tell every single living person he's ever met about something as awesome as flying an F15?

We all passed, though. I spent the entire time bugging my parents about getting tickets to the Moody Blues concert. I also bored them with details about how every person in Israel loves the Stones and thinks Steel Wheels is the best album ever recorded. If you're going to lie, you might as well make it fun.

CHAPTER FOURTEEN – MEET THE BAD GUYS

We were surrounded by dead bodies. The room was in shambles. It had been some sort of restaurant, but now the windows were all blown out and there was busted glass everywhere. A car was burning outside, and the smoke made it impossible to see all the way out to the street. I was standing a few feet in front of Zippy, and a little off to her left. The scary man was in front of me. He was Middle-Eastern, and he was huge. He held a gun in his right hand. His left was held out towards me, with a semi-smile on his face.

"Take my hand, and I will make sure nobody harms you." I was terrified of him. He was evil. I knew it. He would kill me if I didn't take his hand. I didn't want to see that smile fall off his face. That would mean death. I had to do what he wanted.

Zippy started shouting at me "Mark! Don't listen to him!! He's Savak!! He's lying. He's going to kill us. Mark, for God's sake!!!!!"

I couldn't help it. I was just so scared. I reached out and took his hand. He pulled me into a half hug. "Good choice, son." He paused for a few seconds before saying "Allah Akbar."

The hand holding the gun suddenly bolted into the air and

BANG!!!!! He'd shot Zippy right in the heart. I tried to scream but no sounds came out. She twitched there on the ground. A pool of blood quickly made its way outward from her body. Her eyes were still open and looking directly at me. With her last dying breath, she whispered "how could you?"

She died right there. Eyes of disgusted judgment staring at me. I felt sick. Now the scream started to come . . .

. . . I woke up thrashing in my bed. It was the third time I'd had that nightmare since we'd arrived in Israel. I don't know why. Maybe it was the reality of terrorist attacks happening right here in this very city. The first time was the second night we were here. What was wrong with me?

Sunday July 22, 1990

Everyone passed the navigation exam. It was ridiculously easy. They gave us a map and dropped each one of us off in a random spot in Tel Aviv, with instructions to be at a cafe outside Dizengoff Mall in one hour. We started at 8 am. Zippy held the record - 20 minutes. Sivan was right behind her at 22. I made it just shy of 40 minutes. Amir came in last at 48.

We returned to M-Gang Headquarters near supper-time, and were told to meet with Sarah at 8 pm in our little discussion room. She came in with an overhead projector, turned it on, and killed the lights. She began explaining to us just who the bad guys were. For a long time there was the PLO. They were the umbrella under which all the other terrorist groups worked.

But after Israel's war with Lebanon about 8 years ago, a group called Hizbollah formed up in the north, and started committing horrible acts from their bases in Bethlehem and Jericho. This group was funded and trained by the governments of Iran and Lebanon. Iran didn't have any real interest in Palestinians. Iran was Persian. Palestinians were Arabs. The two have historically not liked each other much. But they apparently hate Israel more than they hate each other, and Iran's group was behind most of the terrorist attacks against Israel over the past few years.

There was another group called Hamas, but their activities were largely limited to a small bit of the southern coastal areas of Israel. They were splintered, untrained, and ineffective, so we were going to be worrying primarily with the Bethlehem bunch.

Zippy and Sivan immediately started asking some pretty in-depth questions about the command, supply, and training structure of the group. Sarah put her hands up as if to tell them both to slow down.

"The difficulty we have right now is that the terrorists have organized themselves into 'cell' groups. Each 'cell' is comprised of a team of terrorists and a leader. None of the cells are ever aware of each other, or each other's activities. They receive their orders, and then go commit their crimes." Sarah was drawing a little diagram on the slide of her overhead projector while speaking, as though she needed a visual in order to keep her thoughts together.

Zippy looked for a moment, gathering her thoughts. Then spoke up "So we have to take out every single front line member of every single cell group, then work our way back?"

Sarah looked amused. "There is absolutely no use whatsoever in going after the lone terrorist, the suicide bomber, or the frontline guys in these groups. They are usually just kids who've been grabbed by the real bad-guys, and bullied into doing something they don't want to do - with the threat of horrific violence towards them or their families if they refuse. The front-line bad guys are there against their own will. The real bad-guys are the leaders and the true-believers in the cell groups." Wow!! I'd seen bullies force kids to do stupid things before. It never occurred to me that we might see the same thing happen in

Israel.

Sarah took out a transparency and put it on the projector. It was a photograph of a man in his late 30s. He was Middle-Eastern, black hair, with a mustache and beard that made him look like the sleazy salesman who got himself killed over a Coke in the first Die Hard movie.

"This is the main bad guy right now. His name is Shamil Hassan. He came around about 10 years ago, right after a mob of criminal thugs took over the Iranian government. He was one of the first major liaisons between Iran and the PLO terror network. When Hizbollah first formed, he was one of the key founders, and their primary Iranian connection. Today, he's the one funneling money and weapons from Iran into this terror network. He's also the one smuggling Iranian agents in to train these cells."

Sivan and Zippy looked like they'd seen the face of the Devil. Sivan whispered "So this is the guy we're here to get."

"No. We can't get to him." Sarah's words seemed to deflate everyone in the room. "Even when we capture or destroy a terror cell, we can't get any info leading to him because he has no direct contact with the individual cells. He has about a half dozen lieutenants do this for him. We don't know all their identities, but we're trying to get to them. Each lieutenant is in charge of approximately four cells. We don't know the exact number of lieutenants or cells. But we have the names of four of his lieutenants."

She switched transparencies. This one had four photographs - three males and one female. All of them looked Middle-Eastern. "These people are our targets. For each leader we capture, we get a chance at finding out either Hassan's whereabouts, or we get info on other lieutenants." She paused, "We also get info on all of the cells that each lieutenant is responsible for, and we can go shut it down."

She pointed to the picture on the upper right hand

corner. "The first lieutenant we'll be going after is this man: Abu Nasser. He was the first major PLO player to meet with Hassan eight years ago. He's been linked to five supermarket car bombings. We believe he's coordinating every cell in the Tel Aviv area. If we get him, we can shut down all the Tel Aviv cells and possibly get intel on the location of Hassan."

The door opened. A scary looking Israeli soldier with a shaved head came in and said "We're ready for them." He was surprisingly soft-spoken. A guy who looked like that should have had a tougher sounding voice.

"Tsipporah, Mark, Sivan, and Rachael: You four are on the Nasser mission. The rest of you are going to be helping Shabak setup a cover in Haifa to go after one of Hassan's couriers. Sha'ul here is going to brief you, and introduce you to the Shabak team. He's going to be your handler for the next week or so." The four of them shrugged and went off with him. They seemed half disappointed that they weren't going after Nasser, but they looked intrigued by the "secret" nature of their mission. Once they were gone, there was just the four of us standing by a table in this room with Sarah.

"Ok, for this mission we've already planned out every detail. It's your job to study these plans and begin practicing them. Nasser is staying at a hotel in one of the more interesting parts of Tel Aviv. He goes down to the restaurant for lunch every day at noon. This is where we'll get him.

"The plan is very simple." She continued as she rolled out a map onto the table in front of us. "Dagan and Cohen will be tourists visiting Israel from the United States. You will sit at a cafe outside the hotel till we signal you that everyone is in place. Then you two will discover that Mark misplaced his wallet, and you will run into the hotel to see if it's still in "your" room. If Nasser is in the restaurant, you will pull the fire alarm and head out front, where you'll stay until you see him. When you see him, you run up to him and ask if he's seen your mom, then you turn and run away like you've seen her and have to get to her."

We both looked at her with confusion on our faces. It couldn't possibly be that easy. "That's it?" Zippy mused.

"This is all you have to do. We will have two agents on the ground to apprehend him. And we'll have four snipers stationed on rooftops around the area to take out anyone who tries to harm you or our agents. As a last resort, they may have to take out Nasser, but we really want him alive. There will be two getaway cars. The one coming up the main street in front of the hotel will collect the agents and Nasser."

She pointed at a parallel street running on the opposite end of the hotel. "Your getaway car will be on this street. I'll drive it myself. Katzav and Stein will return with the snipers."

She stepped back. We all seemed to understand our mission pretty well. "Okay, now we need to practice. We will rehearse this at least four times tomorrow. This mission is all you will practice for, and all you will train on until the day we conduct it."

We all understood and we were all ready to start. It just seemed a little overkill for us to practice going into a hotel and pulling the fire alarm and walking back out. Of course it wasn't that easy. We practiced variations where he didn't come out as planned, or where his bodyguards got in our way, or where the hotel's staff caught us pulling the alarm. But we always managed to complete our mission successfully.

I realized around this time that we weren't just going "undercover" as "secret agents" going after some super-villain like in a movie. These were real people. They really would hurt us if they got the chance. They had names. They had friends. They had moms and dads . . sometimes wives and kids. This was real.

I just wanted to avoid the eyes of disgusted judgment. The little fear that my bad dreams had instilled in me stayed in the back of my mind the whole time we were rehearsing our mission. What if something goes wrong? What if Zippy gets hurt, and I could have done something to stop it? What if my nightmares come true?

CHAPTER FIFTEEN – A CHANGE OF PLANS

Saturday, July 28th, 1990

The big day - our first live mission. Zippy, Rachael, Sivan, and I went to breakfast together that morning. We were on "workout blackout," so we didn't get to go to Wingate with the other four M-Gangers. Their mission was a few days away, so they were still training pretty hard. I didn't think it could possibly be any easier than ours, because we didn't have to do much of anything at all. The Alephs from Shabak were doing the hard stuff.

We were all four still nervous as hell. The breakfast they gave us was weird, but it was perfect for what we had to do - blueberries, almonds, olives, and eggs. There was no dairy because that might cause us to cramp, and because Jews can't mix dairy and meat. There was also no bread, noodles, pasta, or anything in that food group because it might slow us down. There was also no talking - not that we were under some oppressive adult supervision or anything. I think we were just all too scared to say anything. Zippy and Rachael finished their breakfast in record time, then went back to looking over the mission plans for the thousandth time. Sivan just looked sullen, like she still felt cheated by Zippy and me getting Beit. I was the last to finish my food, as always.

After breakfast, we all got dressed for the mission. Zippy and I were supposed to be American tourists, so I wore a big oversized T-Shirt with Israel's flag on it, just like all the American tourists you see ALL OVER THE PLACE. I also had on acid-washed blue jeans with the bottoms rolled part way up, and a pair of those sneakers with the lousy air-pumps in them. One of the Mossad chicks helped me get my hair looking all Vanilla Ice. I looked like a clown.

Zippy didn't fare much better. They used an iron to "crimp" her hair into all these weird looking shapes. She had on HUGE oversized earrings, a poofy shirt with an even poofier jacket that had shoulder pads in it, and the shortest shorts known to man. She also had these boyish looking shiny black shoes with white tube socks on.

I thought she looked hot, but you could tell she felt absolutely ridiculous in this getup, and that alone made her look . . . off.

If their goal was to make our looks scream "STUPID TOURISTS", they certainly succeeded.

At 10 in the morning, we all piled into a van and headed out towards the outer parts of town. The plan was to catch Nasser right at lunchtime. We knew this because we'd rehearsed it about 12,000 times.

Zippy and I were dropped off at an outdoor cafe across the street. We found the best table for waiting, ordered juice drinks, and started playing cards while listening to the communication pieces which had been stuffed down into our ears. They were called "coms" for short.

Part of it was unbearably exciting - the anticipation of doing an actual mission and taking down a real bad guy.

The other part was mind-numbingly boring. It was now 10:45, and we had to sit here till our signal to go in, which was scheduled to happen around 12:30. Ugh.

Fortunately, Zippy came prepared with a deck of cards. We were in the middle of a poker hand when the coms crackled. It was Sivan.

"We've got a major problem! Sarah just said that some of the Shabak guys spotted Nasser getting into a car several blocks from here. He's not in the hotel restaurant. He's ON HIS WAY."

Zippy slowly started putting the cards back in the little carrying box, "Do we abort mission?"

"Hang on. I don't know."

That would be aggravating, but I've heard that it happens all the time. If they think there's even a remote chance something might go wrong, the IDF guys will pull the plug in a heartbeat. Of course, when you're sitting there waiting for instructions, it seems like a few million heartbeats.

They wouldn't abort now, would they? The Matkal snipers were all in place. Shabak had a half dozen units in the surrounding neighborhoods ready to swoop in. Mossad spent countless hours watching this guy for us, and the Alephs were already on the scene waiting for Zippy and me to give the signal.

"We're still on." Never thought I'd be so glad to hear Sivan's joyless voice. "But the plan has to change. You're going to tag him outside, and the Alephs are going to get him right after you tag him - no distractions, no misdirection."

So far, so good . . . but after she said that, it was silent for a few seconds longer than I was comfortable with . . something else was wrong.

"There's another problem, Dagan."

"Go ahead, Katzav."

"The signal's no good anymore. You can't tag him like

we practiced. He's not going to be exiting with panicky hotel guests, and your 'where's my mom' thing isn't going to fly without the panic and confusion surrounding you. You've got to get close while he's stepping out of the car, and you've got to signal that it's really him right out there in the open."

She was right. We had to change this one on our feet. The Aleph's wouldn't have to play it much differently, but we'd need to get close outside, and signal right in front of Nasser without him knowing it was a signal.

"I know that, Katzav. I'm not an idiot. You're the Het on this. Tell us what to do."

There was silence for a second. I was getting a bit scared. Not only were we scrapping basically everything we'd practiced, but we were letting Sivan give us instructions. I had no doubt she was trying to figure out a way to get me killed with this little scheme of hers. There was a crackle in both our ears.

"Lover's quarrel."

Zippy suddenly looked angry.

"Say again."

"Lover's quarrel. You're a couple and you're so pissed you're going to break up with him. You storm off and he follows. You shout at him to quit following. Sell it. That should let you get close enough"

Now Zippy was REALLY annoyed. "The SIGNAL Katzav! We've only got a few seconds left!!"

"Oh, yeah . . ." She sounded way too pleased with herself - "if it's Nasser, you turn around and slap Mark as hard as you can. If it's not him, you keep walking."

"Try again Sivan. We're not here for you to take out your personal grudge against-"

"You have your signal, Tsipporah."

Great. Maybe Zippy would take it easy on me - yeah right.

She looked at me with a sudden urgency. "Do you have

any wax on you?"

Oh, no. I knew exactly what she was talking about. She was going to slap me REALLY hard, and it would probably be enough to . . . oh boy, and I didn't have any wax.

"No."

She paused for a few seconds. "Guards are coming out of the building already. The car must be close . . . I'm really sorry Mark." She looked genuinely sad. "Ok, let's make the best of it . . ." She took a few moments with her eyes closed, then suddenly looked both enraged and mischievous at the same time. "You were kissing Sivan weren't you!!!!!! Don't deny it you two-timing swine!!! You were making out with Sivan!!!! What, you just got a thing for Mizrahi girls????"

I was both shocked, horrified, and at the same time I had to nearly bite my lip to keep from bursting out laughing. The next message over coms didn't help either.

"Um . . . trying to keep my food down, guys." Apparently, Sivan didn't find this as amusing as we did.

"What, you've got to stick your tongue in every Mizrahi chick's mouth???"

I had to pull it together, cause if I started laughing now, it was all blown. "Sorry babe, what can I say, she's hot. And she came on to me, not the other way around. She was butterfly kissing me with those upside-down lashes of hers and-"

Zippy shot up from her chair. "You WERE making out with Sivan!!!!!"

Our coms crackled again, "I'm gonna be sick."

"Baby, she meant nothing, and she's nowhere near the kisser that you are. I'll make it up to you next time." I was trying. This crap sounded SO fake coming out of my mouth. I'd never talked like this before. "Let me take you out to the-"

"There WON'T BE A NEXT TIME!!!! We're through, you swine!!!!" She stormed off shouting things in a combination of Hebrew and Arabic which tipped me off to two things. One - she was cussing. Two - she wanted me to shut up because my 'baby, I love you' talk sounded as stupid as it felt. She also timed her stride to just barely keep up with this one particular van that I'd otherwise never have noticed.

The coms buzzed again. "For the record Cohen, I'm the better kisser - not that you'll EVER know. And you're both dead when we get back."

The van came to a stop about 30 feet in front of her, and three guys stepped out of the back. She continued cussing in Hebrew, and everyone in the area was turning around, staring at us, and gasping at what they'd heard. She was slowed just a bit . . just as she walked right into the guy we believed to be Nasser.

"Slikha Bevakisha!!!!!!" She shouted, acting like she was going to shove him for a second. The three guys didn't know what to make of her. I kept walking towards her as quickly as I could. She kept ranting in Hebrew. I just kept trying to get closer to her, in case something started to go down.

She turned around, kept shouting at me, and SMACK!!!!!!! She slapped me so hard it spun my head sideways. She'd put her whole body into the slap. I stood there stunned. I looked at her with my jaw half dropped. Everyone within 50 feet gasped, utterly horrified at what they'd just seen.

This wasn't a normal slap in the face. This was brutal. I tasted blood filling my mouth – damn!!! She hit me so hard that my braces ripped up the inside of my cheeks. Blood was also on my lips. I reached up and touched my quivering lower lip. Yep - blood on the fingers. I looked at Zippy. I couldn't say anything. I just stood there like a statue.

She hissed some foreign profanities at me again, spit at the ground in front of me, and stormed off past three rather amused Mid-Eastern bad guys. I hope Sivan was happy. There was definitely a lump in my throat. Even though I know Zippy didn't mean any of it, the mere shock of getting hit that hard and bleeding into my mouth shook me.

The coms crackled "Get out of there Cohen, it's going down!!!" I stood there, watching Zippy walk the other way, still stunned, shocked, and "Cohen, WAKE UP!!!! Get the hell out of there!!!" Sivan wasn't messing around anymore. I was in danger and she really needed for me to get out of there. The Alephs were probably right behind me.

Scratch that. They were right next to me, walking directly towards Nasser!!!! I turned around and walked away slowly. I didn't want to raise suspicion. SPLAT SPLAT SPLAT!!! I turned around and saw the bodyguards slumping to the ground. Our snipers had taken them all out. The Alephs were right on top of Nasser. I saw the Shabak van speeding up the street towards them. "Cohen, hurry!!!!!" I turned my back on the whole scene and picked up the pace. Is this how secret missions go? Get slapped by the girl of your dreams and let someone else get the bad guy? That never happened to James Bond.

The coms crackled again. It was Rachael. "Mark, turn right into the alley at the next corner and RUN!!! The car will get you at the end of the alley. It's about to get nasty where you are. Tsipporah, you're about to have a fight on your hands. A bunch of kids just shouted "Angel of Death" in Arabic while pointing at you. Two guys are following you very quickly."

"I'm on it." That's Zippy for you. She's not afraid of anything.

"Negative Dagan." Sarah Interrupted. "The snipers have you covered. Let them do their jobs. Don't turn at the next corner as planned. Just keep going straight. Don't turn until Rachel tells you to."

"Got it."

I hit the corner, turned and BOLTED. I got to the end

of the alley about 15 seconds before the car arrived. As I was getting in, I heard a series of cracking sounds. I guess the snipers killed the guys who were tailing Zippy.

"You're clear, Dagan. Take your next left and RUN!!!!"

I wasn't even buckled in, but the car went into a hard reverse. We sped down the street at a nightmarish pace, nearly plowing right into Zippy as she got to her pickup point.

She jumped into the car and we all sped off. Sarah was driving insanely fast, but we HAD to get out of that neighborhood. It was about to become a dangerous place to be. Zippy saw the blood on my lips and instantly went into protective mode.

"Oh my. I'm so sorry Mark. Let me look." She grabbed my face and looked into my mouth. "Here . . ." She ripped a piece of cloth from the bottom of her shirt.

". . . put this in till we can get some wax over your braces." I stuffed the cotton into the side of my mouth. The blood was getting messy. Zippy was pissed. "Sivan's going to pay for this."

"Tsipporah!!!" Sarah didn't sound amused. "Katzav will answer to me, not you. You did your job. What she ordered was a perfectly viable signal. And the mission was a success, which is the only way we judge whether it was the right thing to do."

"Sarah, you didn't see the look on Mark's face while he was just standing there."

"Yes I did, Dagan. It was a mistake because it was not rehearsed. We never do anything which may stun, shock, or otherwise hurt a member of our team unless it is REHEARSED, and you didn't rehearse this one. For that, Sivan is in trouble. Otherwise, you all did your jobs, and nobody got seriously hurt."

"Nobody but Mark."

"A few cuts in the mouth is nothing. Worst case, he gets stitches inside his cheek and goes on antibiotics.

Nobody got shot, stabbed, or had any bones broken. Like I said, Sivan screwed up. And I think she realized that when Mark just stood there after she said for him to move. You should have seen her panicking while I was heading for the car. She might not like Mark, but she doesn't want to see him get hurt or killed, and she REALLY doesn't want to be the cause."

Part of me felt a lot better hearing that. Part of me didn't quite buy it. I couldn't imagine Sivan caring about anything or anyone.

We got back to M-Gang and told the others all about it the mission. We'd gotten the bad guy, and we got away. I had to stop by the infirmary and get the inside of my cheek looked at. They gave me some medicine to put on it, which numbed it whenever it would hurt. I'd have to put wax on my braces for the next week or so, but I'd be alright unless it got infected.

Sarah warned the four of us that right after a mission, when the adrenaline wears off, you experience a crash. It's like you have no energy at all, and you have to fight to keep your eyes open.

Oh did that crash ever hit!!!!!!! It was my night to call my parents. I think we spoke for about 5 minutes. I told them we'd had a particularly hard day of sports and working out. They bought it. I promised we'd talk longer next time I call. They promised they'd actually buy the Moody Blues tickets before the next call. After hanging up, I made it to my room. I know I also made it to my bed because that's where I woke up the next day . . . still in my clothes.

Sunday, July 29th, 1990

So Shabak had this rule: after a mission, you have to have some "decompression" time. For adults in Shabak or Mossad, that means months of talking to shrinks. For M-Gangers, that means a week off. You get your firearm practice for one hour in the morning, your Krav Maga training for one hour in the evenings, and you pretty much have the rest of your time to yourself. We spent a lot of time in the pool, with various tapes blaring out at any given time.

Rachel put together this drink that we all loved. She'd left some bananas and strawberries in the freezer till they were rock hard, then she threw them in a blender with some instant lemonade mix. It tasted like a Sweet-Tart candy flavored slush.

Twice a week, we'd head out to Dizengoff Mall in Tel Aviv to hang out. This had happened since we first arrived in Israel, but these visits just seemed to turn silly after our first live mission.

Zippy and I were inseparable during these trips.

We didn't speak much to Sheri, Danny, Amir or Aaron. Their first mission was 2 days away. We wouldn't know what their mission was till after it was over, but when they heard about the guys chasing Zippy after our mission, they seemed to get a little more nervous about theirs.

The only people who weren't affected one way or another by our missions were Amir and Sivan. Amir would put on his best "tough guy" face, and Sivan was . . . well, she was Sivan. Did she ever smile?

The only downside of this week was that each of us had to meet with a counselor three times for one-hour sessions to make sure we weren't coming "unhinged" by what we'd seen or taken part in. Maybe this stuff really affects the adults or something, but I was living every boy's dream - hanging out with my best friends and a really awesome girl on one day, doing secret missions for the government on the next. Why the hell would anyone need a counselor to get you through this?

CHAPTER SIXTEEN – DARKNESS INTRUDES

Wednesday, August 1st, 1990

I hated those quiet moments that I occasionally had to myself, almost as much as I hated calling home. Nothing against my parents . . . ok, not MUCH against my parents (and I absolutely loved my little sister), but I utterly hated being reminded that Plano was still there. I hated thinking about the city. I hated thinking about my parents' house. I hated thinking about my parents' church. But most of all, my mind kept going back to that place where so many terrible things had happened - the boy's locker room at Anderson Middle School. That was my own personal hell. I guess a small part of me died there, and that's why my mind kept going back, trying to retrieve what had been lost. But it was torture whenever an image of that wretched place would come into my mind. I wanted to drive it out of my head with a drill bit.

I'd gone two months without anyone calling me a "fag." I'd gone two months without having to hear anyone making slurping sounds to taunt me as I'd walk by. I'd gone two months without the giggling whispers in the hallway. I'd gone two months without getting spit at. I'd gone two months without anyone grabbing me while laughing and saying "fairy dust" or some crap like that. It had been two whole months of friends and fun.

I was comfortable, and I was happy. That was the real difference - I was HAPPY. It was like the first couple of months of this wretched year were a bad dream and I'd found this new world where it couldn't touch me. I wanted this trip to Israel to last forever. If I could have signed up and joined the adult Mossad full time, I would have. This wasn't a vacation. This wasn't a training retreat. This wasn't even a mission. This was a new life, and temporary though it may have been, I LOVED IT.

But there was a terrible thing stalking me - August 27th. That was to be the first day of school. That would be the day all of this would end, and all the darkness would come rushing back to drown my life again. Fortunately, I didn't have much time to dwell on that. Constant training does that to you. But in the quiet moments, I'd occasionally think about it. And whenever I'd call home . . . yeah. Everyone in my family seemed to get some sick pleasure out of constantly reminding me that "back to school is just around the corner." I hated calling home. I hated it!!!!!

But it was a necessary evil. M-Gang required parental cooperation, so it was our duty to call home once every 4 days. And guess what tonight was . . . ugh. At least this call would allow me to confirm that my parents had actually bought the Moody Blues tickets. If I was going to have to go back to hell, at least I could have a concert by my favorite band to look forward to.

"Hi Mom."

"Mark!" It wasn't the 'happy to hear you" voice. It was the 'you're in trouble' voice. Here we go . . . "we need to talk."

I managed to keep from uttering a profanity. "What's going on?"

"I had a long conversation with your principal today."

Oh, this was going to suck.

"Did you talk to her about-"

"She wants to put you in with the emotionally disturbed class!!!" Oh wow, the ED kids. They were a special class which was always together all day long. They were also the worst of the worst - usually violent. And my principal had apparently decided to make "a problem" go away by sweeping me under the rug, and right into this group: typical Plano ISD Principal. This was about as bad as it could get.

"Mom, you know I don't belong-"

"Mark, that doesn't matter!!! The decision is made. She's going to put you in there unless you go and beg. You need to admit that you did something wrong, and promise to do-"

"Mom I didn't do anything wrong!!! Two kids made up a story about me. That's all. That's the beginning and end of it. Everyone believes that story because they want to. It's fun to them."

She paused for a few seconds. "Well, you have to have done something." There's a Catholic parent for you - it's always at least SOME your fault, no matter what. "People don't just decide to pick on you for no reason. And you should know your father is talking about sending you to San Marcos Military Academy."

I felt this explosion of rage, fear, and disgust in my chest. My father had been talking about that for years. It was his typical threat, "Shape up, or military school will beat you into shape." Brilliant.

And he was back to threatening that one again. But this time it would mean that I'd NEVER see the M-Gang kids. If I couldn't train with them in Dallas, I couldn't be part of the program. No more Zippy. To say the least, our conversation got a bit more heated after that. We went back and forth between me explaining that my principal wasn't going to listen to me and my mother stubbornly insisting that she would. After a few minutes, the conversation degraded into a simple "yes she will - no she won't" back and forth. Finally, I think we'd both had enough.

"She WON'T LISTEN, mom. YOU won't even listen. How can I expect her to. You want me to take the 'responsibility' for the things that happened to me. I'm not going to do that. Just . . . let me talk to Dad."

She handed him the phone, but his response wasn't much better. "We'll work this out, Mark. It may be VERY hard, but we'll work it out." I got a small level of comfort from his voice tone. It told me he wasn't REALLY thinking about sending me to San Marcos. He was just as frustrated with the situation as I was.

We talked for a few minutes, but he wouldn't get any more specific than "we'll see what happens." I really needed a solution, but all I was going to get from this conversation was questions. Would I end up in ED? Would I have to go to Principal Samson begging? Would I have to worry about military school?

Worst of all, I had to let this impending nightmare gnaw at me HERE, the one place on Earth where I thought I could be away from it. I just felt SO ANGRY.

"Fine, I've gotta go."

I hung up the phone . . okay, I SLAMMED it down, but who's getting hung up on semantics? I stood there for a few seconds, trying my best to hold back the tears, but they were too strong. I choked for a second, then started to cry. The darkness had tracked me down all the way to Tel Aviv. I so wanted to just blink and make the whole Anderson nightmare go away. I did my best to gather myself up, turned around, and walked right into Sivan. Oh this was just getting better and better.

"Sorry Katzav. Didn't realize you were there."

"It's . . . ok . . Cohen." She was giving me a rather odd look. "I was here for some time . . . and I'm sorry. When I heard about this last spring, I thought it was . . exaggerated. I didn't know."

I didn't know what else to say - "Thank you."

"It's what Mizrahim have faced. Sephardim too. It's what I went through in elementary school. I was afraid to go to school because other kids would gang up on the Persian girl. I understand, Cohen."

And just in case you thought the moment was about to get too sentimental as she moved towards the phone . . .

"Of course, you still suck as an M-Ganger." She smiled. WOW, Sivan actually CAN smile. ". . . but I know what you go through, and I'm sorry . . . and if there is a time or a way I can help, I will."

And with that, she took the phone and dialed up her mom, who was visiting her relatives in Haifa for a few days. "Imeh. Zeh Ani. Manishmah HaYom?"

I really needed to work on my Hebrew.

I went back to my room and tried to brainstorm a way that I could stay in Israel. Hmmm . . . I could convert to Judaism, contact an Ayliah organization . . . I could apply for asylum . . . I could . . . there was a knock at my door.

It was Zippy. She had that serious look on her face again.

"Hey . . Sivan told me." She burst into the room. "I want you to know that no matter what, when we say 'never again' we mean it. There are two other M-Gangers at Anderson, and we will NOT let those things happen to you again. We also have . . . influence in things. You will not end up with ED kids, even if I have to frame your principal for child molestation."

She'd do it, too.

"Thanks Zippy, but I'm not sure what-"

"Or you could come to D'var Adonai."

A light went on in my head. I might be able to go to school with Zippy and her closest friends!!!! "Are you serious? That's for Jewish k-"

"My family can make it happen. It won't be easy, but we can talk to them. I'll ask my parents to contact yours and see if they're open." She didn't let me respond, she just got up and walked out.

I didn't know what to feel. Nothing had really happened to make me feel better. I was still slated to go to Anderson, and still slated to be stuck in the ED class, but the mere fact that Zippy had come up with a practical way out . . . there was hope in my heart after all. Suddenly, August 27th didn't look so bad. It might downright be something to look forward to.

Thursday, August 2nd, 1990

As if going back to school in a few weeks weren't already hanging over my head, today the entire M-Gang visit to Israel went wrong. We all woke up, did our morning Krav training and shooting drills, then everything went sideways. Saddam Hussein, the President of Iraq, decided to invade Kuwait. Yep, I was in Israel, and a war was breaking out a few hundred miles away.

Mossad was going nuts all around us, and none of the adults we were supposed to be working with were available. Nobody had time for the kids, so we just sat in the lounge and watched the whole thing on CNN. Everyone wanted to know everything about Iraq. And they wanted to know it all yesterday. After a few hours, we eventually gave up on the TV and went over to our spot at Wingate for some training time. And without any adults to get in the way, Zippy led one of the most intense Krav and sparring sessions we'd had in weeks. After about an hour and 45 minutes, Sarah came through the door and had us gather round.

"This changes everything for Mossad, and it changes everything for the politicians and the military. But it changes nothing for Shabak, and it changes nothing for you. This team's mission is still Hassan's network."

You could almost feel a sigh of relief going through the eight of us. We were all afraid she was going to say our mission was off, and we were all going home or something.

"All eyes are going to be on Iraq for the foreseeable future, and this is very dangerous because nobody is going to be looking at Iran. Iran is still our greatest threat. The terrorist groups in the Bethlehem area are still getting support and supplies from Iran. We HAVE to disrupt this, and now is the perfect time. They think they have a free pass because everyone is gearing up to worry about Iraq. We have a unique opportunity to go after some of Hassan's top guys over the next two weeks, and we intend to use you kids to do it."

The energy level in our little group must have gone up at least three notches with those words.

"Our next target is Adara Salimah. She's known as the 'black widow.' She's Jordanian, 24 years old, and has been working as one of Hassan's coordinators since Israel neutralized her fiancé about 2 years ago. He'd been one of Hassan's sidekicks, and she basically took his place. Here is her photograph."

I remembered her picture from the slide of bad-guys Sarah showed during one of our earlier meetings. Was it just me or were all Middle-Eastern girls impossibly gorgeous? The picture looking back at me could have just as easily been one of the Mizrahi chicks at Wingate. I couldn't believe how beautiful she was.

"We cannot get close to her like we did with Nasser. She's amazing at spotting agents. The last one who got close to her was a Matkal guy working undercover with Shabak. He underestimated her close-quarters hand to hand combat abilities, and found himself naked and bound to a chair where she proceeded to slice him up. Our forensic guys estimate she was cutting on him for days before he bled out, and every cut was meant to maximize the agony, rather than to do real damage to the body. A bodyguard we captured not long after said she never even asked the poor guy a single question. She just wanted to refine her torture technique with a blade."

Oh wow. And people like this exist. I looked over at Zippy. She had the predator look in her eyes. Behind her stood Sheri and Danny, holding each other's hands so tightly I thought one of them would crush the other.

"I should also warn you. We believe she's responsible for a school-bus bombing, so she'll have no difficulties killing a kid. You guys are going to be in some real danger on this one. We believe we know where she'll be in 2 days, so you won't have much time to rehearse the op. The Sayerets are all focusing on the Iraq thing, and most of Mossad's agents are gearing up to head off on missions in that area. Shabak is on full alert . . . so that means this one is an M-Gang only mission. Are there any questions?"

Zippy's hand shot straight up. "Are we going to poison, bomb, shoot, get personal, or take her alive?"

"Yes."

CHAPTER SEVENTEEN – DISASTROUS SUCCESS

Friday, August 10th, 1990

Sarah's superiors were a little hesitant about our Salimah mission, but she rammed it down their throats. She was particularly keen on catching this particular bad guy . . er, girl, and we spent every minute preparing for our mission. We had no idea why this was so special to Sarah, but we were happy to oblige. It was all hands on deck. All eight M-Gangers were onboard.

Adara Salimah was evil incarnate. But she was getting careless. We knew exactly which hotel she was staying at. We knew which restaurant she was going to be eating at. Either she was setting a trap for the next Israeli counter-terror team, or she was making a critical error. Since neither Shabak, Mossad, nor Matkal had enough manpower to devote to catching her, M-Gang got the job.

Since we were short-staffed, M-Gang got to assign Alephs on this one too. Zippy and Amir took Aleph. Danny and I took Beit. Aaron and Sheri got Het. It would have been Sivan, but after her last experience with Het, she asked to be anything but Het again. So she and Rachael shared Ayin.

Some of us decided very quickly that we couldn't take this monster alive, so Zippy planned one kill and Amir planned another kill. Danny and I were to cover them at the same time. However, when Sarah heard about the plan, she insisted on joining as a third Aleph, with her job being to capture Salimah alive. This made life especially interesting for Danny and me. We now had three Alephs to cover, and one of them was our adult handler.

Zippy was going to slip poison in Salimah's food - an idea which she thought was the best because it allowed us to do the mission with the least contact. Since Salimah was so dangerous, and had killed operatives who'd gone after her before, taking her without any contact seemed like the safest route.

Amir was going to place a bomb under her bed - an idea he took from all the "Operation: Wrath of God" missions we'd read about. This also had the advantage of minimal contact. We just had to slip into her room, avoid any booby-traps, slip back out undetected, then catch her sleeping.

Sarah was going to go in after the poison had begun to incapacitate her, but before she could get back to her room. Sarah wanted to try to capture her as she was falling unconscious, then get her some medical attention before the poison could kill her. She was more valuable to us alive than dead.

Little did Sarah know that Zippy planned to use Tetrodotoxin, which had no known antidote, and was more deadly than cyanide. It had a delayed reaction, kicking in about 20 minutes after exposure. This meant that even if Salimah used a guard to test her food, he wouldn't show any symptoms until after she'd ingested her poisoned food.

Zippy and Amir also hatched a backup scheme to move

in on Salimah's hotel room with guns drawn if all other plans failed.

Since this was all taking place inside a hotel, we had no sniper cover, and the Ayins had to guide us out using blueprints only - definitely not the preferred scenario. The Hets also had to control the operation blind, which basically left operations in the hands of the Alephs and Beits.

Shabak would have never gone forward with it. They'd have said the plan was too complicated, and that we should just let the Matkals go in guns blazing from the start. But we weren't Shabak or Special Forces. We were M-Gang, and this was our plan.

Sarah checked us into a room in the hotel. From there, we spent about a day walking around, getting a feel for the place. It was the typical Tel Aviv hotel. Zippy spent most of her time hanging around the restaurant, and being an annoying kid with too many questions for the wait staff. She made up this great story about wanting to be a chef.

She was good.

After a few hours, she'd sweet-talked her way into a full tour of the kitchen, and she'd gotten to talk to the main chef, the saucier, and the pastry-chef. The main chef was going to be busy working on a special fish dinner that evening, but he said Zippy could either sit at the soup station or watch the saucier work with some bizarre concoction he was cooking up. If she'd stayed under-cover on this mission long enough, she'd have learned enough tricks to make herself a pretty good chef - if the assassin thing didn't work out for her.

Of course, she wasn't really there to learn food. She was there looking for the best opportunity to slip a slightly bitter-tasting poison into whichever of Adara Salimah's orders would be most likely to conceal the taste. She finally radio'd in that this was going to be a long shot.

Danny and I spent the day watching Salimah's bodyguards. They had her room pretty well covered.

There were three guards: one on each end of the hall where her room was, and one in the lobby at all times. This wasn't going to be easy.

Our rehearsals hadn't included the guards being inside the hotel while Salimah was out, and it's hard to plant a bomb in someone's hotel room when they've got guards constantly watching it. Fortunately, we didn't have to figure it out. Aaron, Sheri and Sarah had been working on a plan in our hotel room. Sarah wanted to abort the mission, but she stuck with us on faith alone. Aaron, Sheri, Zippy, Amir and I were all so adamant that we could do this, she couldn't help be convinced.

But we were also running out of time. Amir needed 5 minutes alone to set and arm the bomb. Then he needed to be able to get out of there unspotted. That meant we probably needed to distract both the guards in the hall for 10 minutes to give him time to get in, get out, and deal with any unexpected problems. How do you distract 2 guards for 10 minutes, and still get them back into their places so that the target isn't alerted that something is wrong?

Sarah suddenly had an idea: the direct approach. That's what the Matkals would do if they were here. It tended to work, so we'd give it a try here - no matter how reckless it may sound. Sarah would distract the guards, but not by trying to be a tourist or some other cover. She'd be an OBVIOUS Shabak agent. She'd get their attention, and they'd watch her long enough to make sure that she's not an immediate threat, then they'd go back to their posts. She'd be a bumbling agent, so they wouldn't be too worried. Zippy was going to be furious - all this action going on upstairs, and she was stuck getting cooking lessons.

My job was to hide in the stairwell and keep an eye on the hallway. Amir was crouched down behind me, waiting for my signal that all was clear. Then he could go running to the doorway, get into Salimah's room, and plant the bomb.

Salimah's room was exactly halfway down the hall between the stairwell and the elevator.

Danny ran downstairs to keep an eye on the restaurant and support Zippy. We all had coms in our ears and were ready to go. It was probably the longest 90 seconds of my life waiting for Sarah to arrive.

The elevator door opened, and out walked Sarah - right past the first of Salimah's bodyguards. She walked halfway down the hall to Salimah's room, and just stood there looking at it. Then she turned, reciting the number of the room repeatedly while walking back towards the elevator.

She couldn't have SCREAMED "I'm a Shabak agent" any louder than that, even if she'd worn a badge around her neck and had a big gun resting on her hip. And oh, she had their attention alright! The guard on our end of the hall whispered something in Arabic into his coms and started towards her. I just hoped Salimah herself didn't have coms on - wherever she was.

My coms buzzed - Rachael was on the other end. "The guard in the hallway just b-lined it to the elevator. He's hitting the button over and over again . . . guys, he's coming up." The guard on our end was walking directly towards Sarah.

Suddenly, Sivan buzzed over the coms "Guys, Salimah is here!!!! She'll be coming through the front door in about 30 seconds. I'll track her that far, then I'm off." The plan was for Sivan to go straight to our room once Salimah entered the building. I was starting to shake, I was so nervous. This was about to get VERY nasty.

Sarah whispered into her coms, "I'm leaving my transmitter on so you'll hear everything. Finish the mission. Don't worry about me." I looked at Sarah. She was nearly to the elevator. The guard next to it was being very nonchalant. The guard from our end was about 5 steps behind her. She made it too the elevator door. It opened.

The other guard was inside!!!!! Sarah started talking,

"Shalom, Ayfo-" He made a stabbing motion into her gut, and her entire body went limp. All three guards pulled her into the elevator. The door began to close behind them.

"Sarah's down!!!! I'm going to rescue her!!!!" Amir yelled as he went charging down the hall towards the elevator. He dropped the bomb right next to me, and pulled his Beretta as he ran. The coms went wild.

"This is Dagan. I'm on my way up the stairs. Mark, have the bomb ready. I'll set it myself. Don't move from where you are!!!!"

Amir struggled with the elevator doors - fighting with every ounce of strength he had to pry at them. I never knew he felt so strongly about Sarah.

"This is Rachael, the elevator stopped on three. Aaron is heading up the stairs to intercept."

Amir finally got the elevator door pried open, and jumped down into the shaft. I managed to pick up all the pieces of his bomb just in time for Zippy to arrive. She grabbed the bomb pieces, whispered a few profanities, yanked the coms out of her ears, stuffing them into her pocket, and then bolted down the hall.

While she was picking the lock to Salimah's room, she yelled back at me "Whatever Sivan says, keep silent."

I don't know what she was expecting, but it couldn't be good. She got the lock picked in about 15 seconds, then disappeared into the room. I just sat there hoping and praying that there were no booby-traps for her to run into.

Sure enough, the coms crackled. "This is Sivan. She's inside. I repeat - Adara Salimah is inside the building, and she's heading to the elevator."

I kept quiet. Zippy had warned me not to say anything.

"Come in Dagan. This is Sivan. She's going straight to the elevator . . . Dagan, come in!!!!!" It was hard keeping quiet, but Zippy knew what she was doing.

"Tsipporah - come in!!!! Tsippi, this is Sivan, come in!!!!! Tsippi, she's getting into the elevator, GET OUT OF

THERE!!!!!" I wanted to say something, but she'd said to keep quiet. "Mark can you see Tsipporah?"

I stayed silent.

"Mark!!!! Come in!!!!"

I couldn't do it anymore. "This is Cohen. Zippy is in Salimah's room. She's gone coms-silent. I'm watching the elevator."

"I'm coming up." Oh boy, this wasn't going to be good. If she came up, then Zippy would know I broke coms silence. She'd totally kick my backside for that..

"Negative Sivan. Stick to the plan. Get to the M-Gang room."

There were suddenly several popping sounds from downstairs. It was the unmistakable sound of gunfire. Amir and Aaron had gotten into a firefight.

"Sivan. Amir and Aaron are engaging the guards on three!!!! Stay downstairs, she's-"

The elevator door opened.

There she was.

Adara Salimah in the flesh!!!

I felt almost starstruck for a moment. She'd let her jet black hair down, and was wearing a black jean jacket, tank-top, and ridiculously short shorts which showed off her frighteningly long legs . . all the way down to the cleopatra sandals. I'd seen pictures of her for days, and always thought she was one of the most beautiful girls I'd ever seen.

She was just as impossibly gorgeous in person as she had been in photos. She also apparently knew how to use that beauty as a weapon. It's little wonder she managed to take out every agent sent after her. My heart ached just looking at her myself. Why oh why oh why did she have to be one of the bad guys? It just didn't seem right. She walked down the hall as though she knew there was someone in the room, and she couldn't wait to take them out. It was like watching a predator. What was worse, she was completely silent. Ballerina-like grace gave her the advantage of the softest footsteps you could ever imagine. She stopped for just a moment before going through the door.

In utter horror, I watched her pull out a knife from a holster hidden behind her belt. Even if I hadn't read her file, I would have instantly known she was an expert by the way she held it. She knew someone was in the room waiting for her, and she was going to go in anyway, which meant she knew exactly where that person was hiding, and what that person was planning. She'd fought Israeli forces for long enough that she had their playbook memorized. Zippy was about to become her next victim!!

She threw open the door and took her first step inside in one move, stabbing forward, and slashing to the sides. Had anyone been hiding out to ambush her behind the door, they'd have been dead. Zippy was probably so focused on the bomb that she wouldn't realize Salimah was there until it was too late.

I didn't think. I jumped up and ran down the hall shouting at the top of my lungs, "Adara!!! Adara Salimah!!!" I veered left into the door and came to a stop 5 feet behind her with my hands out as though I wanted a hug.

She turned and looked right at me with same expressionless face I'd seen in all her photos. My goodness, she was beautiful!!!! I just stood there. I don't know what I was expecting. Did I really think she'd take one look at me and feel any differently than with anyone else she'd killed? Did I expect her to crack a smile on that dead face of hers and say "hi there, want to come inside" or something? She took a sudden step towards me faster than I could blink.

FLASH!!!

I felt an explosion of pain in my tummy, shooting all the way up to my heart. The kick had been so lightning fast I hadn't even seen it. She'd nailed me with a Zippy-style groin kick. My entire upper body automatically slumped over, which may very well have saved my life because Salimah missed me altogether when she shot in with the knife. I started puking from the shocking pain. She slashed the knife across my chest before I could completely fall forward. The fire screamed across my ribcage, just as my legs gave out from under me. I was seriously in trouble.

She grabbed me by the hair with her left hand, and jerked my head back. I was vomiting uncontrollably. Puke was spewing everywhere, but it didn't faze her a bit. I looked into her soulless eyes for a split second. She placed the knife right at my throat to slash. She was going to murder me with no thought or emotion. The look on her face was completely dead. She could have just as easily been turning the page on her wall calendar as slitting a kid's throat.

SPLAT!!!! Her head exploded right in front of me, spraying blood all over my face. The hand holding the knife relaxed as the entire body went limp standing there. I continued to slump to the floor. SPLAT SPLAT SPLAT, her chest kept exploding in various places. Zippy was standing about 10 feet to my right, emptying her P88 into Salimah. She kept firing as she walked closer.

I crumbled into the fetal position. The pain was overwhelming. My whole body had tightened up and I just kept rolling back and forth. The slash across my chest made it even worse. Zippy emptied an entire clip into Salimah by the time she'd walked up to the body on the floor. Then she changed clips, and fired a few more shots into what had been Salimah's head. She made sure the room was clear, then came over to help me.

Our coms crackled - it was Amir. "We neutralized the guards on three. Sarah's not injured, but she's dazed and too messed up to walk. They hit her with a stun gun. We're going to get her to the room."

"Got it. I'll cover the hallway," said Sivan in a complete

monotone voice.

Zippy fumbled for her coms, "Cohen's down, and going into shock. He's going to need a medic. Somebody prep an ice pack and some gauze for me. I'm going to try to get him to the room." She paused like she'd forgotten something. "Oh . . and mission successful. We killed Salimah. I repeat - Adara Salimah is dead."

I hadn't been able to take a complete breath of air since taking the groin shot - my lungs and diaphragm had been spasming so hard. I didn't realize it till I started tunnel visioning. Zippy was rolling me over to try and stand me up, just as I passed out. Oh well . . .

CHAPTER EIGHTEEN – CAN THIS GET ANY WORSE

I woke up in a bed in a hotel room. I was shivering. There was a makeshift bandage across my ribs, and an . . . hang on a minute . . . there was an ICE PACK down in between my legs. No wonder I was shivering. What idiot put that there? I reached down to pick it up and heard Sarah's voice. "Don't mess with it, Cohen."

She got up from her chair and walked over to my bed side. "It's getting rid of the swelling for you."

Oh boy. I suddenly remembered. How badly was I injured? Would I still be able to have kids? I felt an intense panic. Sarah must have noticed.

"You'll be glad to know that nothing's broken or ruptured. You're going to be fine." I didn't even ask how they knew that. I was just thrilled to hear it. The pain was already coming back . . BIGTIME, despite the ice pack. "You're a lucky boy. Zippy said it looked like a life changer when Salimah kicked you." She smiled. "But you being there accomplished the Beit's job perfectly. It bought Zippy the second she needed to draw her weapon."

She leaned in and whispered, "But don't you EVER do that again. Distract a target if you must. But don't let yourself get taken like that. If Zippy had been a fraction of a second slower, you'd be in a body bag, and I'd be out of a job. As it is, I've got enough questions to answer from angry people asking about what kind of program we're running here. Fortunately, I can tell them that nobody was seriously injured, and we just had a kid collect a minor cut and some bruises."

She stood back up straight. "That's another way that you're criminally lucky." She pointed at the bandage across my ribs. "She was well trained to just barely poke with the knife and slash upwards at an angle - just like we are. But when she stabbed, you were already slumping over, and the 'poke" didn't even touch your skin. I guess she thought you could handle her kick better than you did. Anyway, your slash wound is only skin deep. Your shirt took most of the damage."

I reached up and touched the bandage. Sarah took my hand and put it back down to my side. "No you don't. You have to wear that bandage for a few days. We're coming up with a cover story for your parents. Right now, we're wanting to say that a cat clawed you, and you threw it off, but one of its claws was stuck in your skin when you did."

"How long have I been out?" Wow my voice sounded weak.

"Quite a while. We gave you a sedative to keep you out. You'd only have been in more pain if we'd let you wake up earlier. But you'll be heading back to M-Gang within the hour. Shabak teams are escorting the M-Gangers out of here two at a time." She laughed a bit, "I sent Dagan downstairs for lunch. She's crawling out of her skin waiting to talk to you. I didn't think it was possible for someone to be so worried."

"I'm sorry I screwed up."

"You didn't screw up, Cohen - not badly anyway. It was a dangerous mission and we got it accomplished. Salimah is dead. Her guards are dead. And we didn't lose anybody. We just ended up with one kid roughed up and an adult with a slight burn on her side." She lifted her shirt a bit to show the burns just under her ribs from the stun gun. "Now, you try to relax. Dagan will be in here to see you in a few minutes."

"When's the next mission?"

She looked at me with absolute incredulity on her face. "Have you COMPLETELY lost whatever mind you had to begin with, you HOPELESSLY STUPID Texan?!?!?!?" Heh . . she sounded like Zippy when she said that. "You're through going on missions for the summer. You're going to have the rest of the week to decompress, then you can relax at M-Gang till the plane comes to get you. It's only 12 days away, or I'd be having you sent home immediately."

"Sarah!!" My voice sounded horribly weak. Exactly what sedative HAD they given me? "Please. We've got enough time to setup another one and get one more of Hassan's guys before we have to go. We won't get another chance at this. You said it yourself - it's all Iraq all the time now. Hassan will have free run to set things up and kill people if we don't get him."

She looked like she was about to cry. She muttered something in Hebrew and walked towards the door. She stopped before opening it, looking at the ground.

"My niece Dana was on a bus full of school children that . . . she was killed by one of Salimah's bombings. She was five, and she was beautiful." Her voice cracked on the last word. She was fighting to not cry in front of me. "They had to identify her from DNA because nothing was left of her little face."

A single tear ran down her cheek. She looked back at me. "When something truly traumatic like that happens in your life, it can . . . it can break your morality. It broke mine. I got so caught up in revenge that I put the lives of children at risk. Adara's got broken as well. She killed children. She truly became a monster. I don't want to become that."

She opened the door, "I should never have approved this mission. I WILL NOT have your blood on my hands. I'm sorry, Mark. I'm no monster. I will not throw you into danger." And with that, she left the room.

Dammit. I thought I could convince her. Maybe Zippy would have more luck. Certainly Zippy would put up an argument for letting us do one more mission.

I spent about ten minutes flipping through channels on the TV. Then the door opened up and Zippy popped her head in. She looked at me for a few seconds, then marched right up to my bedside. The look on her face an equal mix of concern and anger.

SMACK!!!!! She slapped me across the side of my head. "You IDIOT!!!!!! How many times did I tell you to NEVER look your opponent in the eyes?!?!?!? Why did she nearly kill you? Because she incapacitated you first! How did she incapacitate you? She kick you - with a kick I WELL trained you to defend against. But no!!!! You reacted too slow and she land the shot. Why? You were no looking center mass on her body. No. You had to be stupid Texas gentleman and look a lady in the eye. AND YOU NEARLY DIE FOR IT!!!!!"

Zippy was absolutely in a rage. SMACK!!!! She hit me again. SMACK! "Stupid!!!!" SMACK!! "Idiotic!!!!" SMACK!!!! "Texan!!!!!"

She was breathing so heavily I thought she might collapse where she stood. "I NO bring you here to get you hurt! You HAVE to be more careful! I no can stand to see you hurt. I love you Mark!"

We both froze.

Did she just say what I think she just said? After a few seconds, I started to open my mouth with no idea what words may be about to come out when . . SMACK!!!!!!

She immediately turned and walked out of the room, slamming the door behind her so hard that the ticking clock fell off the wall and shattered on the floor. I'm so glad nobody else was here when she said that. We'd never hear the end of it.

This was turning into a rather weird day. I got back to M-Gang . . . ok, I LIMPED back into M-Gang. I was in considerable pain. She'd only hit me once, and it was only a kick. I couldn't imagine how horrible it would be to take that series of knees that Zippy was so fond of delivering during training. Some of the kids congratulated me, but they all seemed to be hiding something sad. I couldn't put my finger on it.

Amir was his usual boisterous self. "How you like this guy, huh? Major terrorist. Such great hand-to-hand skills that shes take out special forces guys. And this guy goes charging in at her UNARMED!!!!!!! Cohen, I think your new name should to be 'Suicide.' No?"

Sivan just shook her head in disgust when she saw me, "You're an idiot, Cohen!!! Next time you want to try getting your balls broken, come to me first. I'll gladly destroy them for you. The ice pack won't save you, but at least I won't slice you up afterwards." She went off to her newly assigned private room. Yes, she and Zippy were given private rooms just before this mission. Apparently the Sabra Sisters were fighting so much that the adults had to separate them. Just before slamming the door behind her, she muttered one last time, "IDIOT."

I sat around watching TV most of the day. Walking hurt too much. Well . . . sitting hurt quite a bit too, but walking was really bad. I got up a few times to go get a snack. I hadn't seen Sarah since the hotel. Then around 3 in the afternoon, I went to our kitchen area to get a snack. As I walked by Sivan's room, I overheard Sarah talking to her.

"You've got to give me better than that, Katzav. I can't go back and say we should keep someone who puts his friend over the mission, just because he lucked into the mission being a success." Oh no. She wasn't kidding back at the hotel. There WERE people above her with questions . . . about ME. That's what the M-Gangers had all been hiding. Someone upstairs wanted me out of the program.

Sivan's responded, "Well, she has this obsession with him. She's been watching him for a very long time."

"I know that."

"No. I mean a VERY long time. She's been watching him for years. But she didn't recruit him till he needed us worse than anything else in the world." What does she know? I'd been Zippy's friend for years. She wasn't watching me. She was hanging out with me.

"Why would she do this?"

Sivan paused, "I'm not sure. At first, I thought that she had a crush on him. But I no longer think this. I think she chose him years ago because he was never popular. His mom was a teacher at his school, and kids would beat him up whenever she give one of their friends a detention. He was always bullied, although never as bad as this last year. He moved to a new school and it got much worse. He made the wrong enemies. And when that got really bad, she suddenly became obsessed with making him into one of us."

After a short pause, Sivan continued, "I think she was using him. I've got no love for that stupid goy, but what she's doing to him is worse than wrong. When I first came to you and tried to get you to remove him, I was trying to protect him. But now she's nearly gotten him killed, and for what? To prove that she's the ultimate agent? That she can recruit someone and mold him into such a perfect and loyal dog that he lay down his life for her? He doesn't deserve to get kicked out. He did exactly what he was meant to do. But he needs to be taught to protect

HIMSELF . . . because right now he only thinks to protect her. I'd tell him as much, but he won't listen."

Sarah took a moment to respond, like she was writing all of this down. "Well, I'm going to talk to Tsippi again in about five minutes. If this is true, then there might be something to take back to them. Otherwise, Cohen is on a plane tomorrow."

I felt sick. Either my best friend was using me, or I was about to get kicked out of M-Gang, lose all my friends, and go home to Plano. This couldn't be real.

I went on to the kitchen and pretended to get a snack. I waited for Sarah to emerge. Sure enough, she slipped out of Sivan's room, and walked straight down the hall to Zippy's.

When I was sure the coast was clear, I headed down the hall, and eavesdropped. Sarah and Zippy were talking in an almost relaxed manner, like this conversation wasn't going to result in whether I get kicked out of M-Gang. They were talking like it was nothing.

"Why Cohen, though?" Sarah sounded genuinely curious.

"It makes sense. He doesn't just fit the profile, he IS the profile. Future recruits should all look just like him . . . on paper anyway. I've recruited several kids to M-Gang now. He's the only one besides me who'll never quit." She sounded like an artist describing her masterwork. I started to feel frightened. I was afraid that I was about to hear something that was going to hurt.

"How do you know?"

There was a pause. Zippy's voice softened, "Because he was defined by his fears. He was raised by parents who are defined by THEIR fears. He was afraid of everything. He would be beaten up by children his own age because he was too afraid to hit back - they might get angrier and beat him harder. Now look at him! He runs into room to confront an armed terrorist without even drawing weapon."

"So you've made him stupid?"

"No!! Don't you get it?? I've taken away his fears!!!! When you take away someone's fear, they love you forever. They absolutely devoted to you. Fanatical even. If you truly want to own someone, pluck their fears from their heart and make sure they understand it was YOU who did it. Governments and religions do this. WE will do this!! And we will have teams of agents who are violently loyal to us. They will lay down their lives for us. They will do anything we ask. And they will thank us for the opportunity to die for our purposes. This is Mark Cohen. This is the perfect agent."

I heard the door to Sivan's room click, so I immediately started walking toward the kitchen again. Better to be looking for a "snack" than to let anyone know I'd heard what I've just heard.

I felt nauseous. All this time. All the things we did. All the things she did for me. It was all a LIE????

I don't think I said a word to anybody during dinner. If Zippy wasn't really my friend, then what was the use of it all? Going back to Anderson and facing that gauntlet every day, getting put in ED and having to worry about getting knived, going off to military school . . . what was the point?

Everyone else seemed happy, though. They all acted like a weight had been lifted off them. After dinner, we all gathered to watch a movie.

I excused myself and went to go put in my obligatory call home. My mind had been wondering the entire evening. Part of me was terrified that Sivan was right about Zippy. But another part of me had secretly concocted this scenario where Zippy had just told Sarah what Sarah needed to hear to keep me in the program.

But I had no way of knowing without asking. And I was too terrified of the answer to ask. I let that thought make me angry as I called home. I really wanted to talk to my parents, but had no idea what I wanted to say.

My mother answered the phone.

"Hi Mom, it's Mark."

"Are you all right???? Your father and I have been worried sick."

"Mom, it's nothing."

"Mark, they're saying that Iraq is going to attack Israel next. I want you home. I want you safe."

"Mom, I'm safe. Nothing is happening here. It's hundreds of miles away. Did the Dagans call you?" Might as well get to the point.

"Yes. Your father wants to talk to you about this." She handed him the phone.

"Hi, Son."

"Hi, Dad."

"What's going on?"

"Did the Dagans call you?"

"Yes they did." He was being obtuse. He was going to make me ask him directly. He always excelled at that.

"And?"

"Mark, we're not going to send you to a Jewish school. Your mother and I are already concerned about the amount of time you spend with these kids."

Un-friggen-believable. "Dad, they're my friends!!!!" I felt so fake saying those words. Were they really my friends? I don't know whether he heard the phoniness in my voice, but it didn't matter.

"We don't think it's healthy for you to spend that much time being influenced by another religion. But we did get an idea. Your mom made a phone call to Collins Christian Academy over in Addison."

I couldn't quite believe what I was hearing. "Huh?"

"We called a private school in Addison and told them about what had been happening to you. They apparently thought you really needed a chance to start over, and they're the perfect place for you to do it."

"But Dad, we can't afford that. The Dagans were going

to set things up for us at D'var Adonai."

"This may require a little belt tightening - less eating out, less renting movies, and no more buying tapes every month." He was talking about it as if these things actually mattered to me anymore. I was costing my parents a lot less money than I did this time last year, and I didn't want him to forget it.

"Well, I've already dropped Tang Soo, and I don't really watch movies anymore since M-Gang, so you won't be spending much on m-"

"I don't want you to worry about that. Just come home safe, and do well on their aptitude test. And by the way, don't worry about the Moody Blues concert. We've already bought the tickets." My blood pressure doubled.

"REALLY?????? Where are we sitting?"

"Right in the middle of the shed. The Dagans are going too, but they're sitting in a different section. So you REALLY have to keep yourself safe for the next two weeks."

I had to wait a few seconds to take it all in before saying it: "Thank you, Dad."

"I love you, son. Just remember - the Lord takes care of fools and children. I'm a fool and you're a child, so between the two of us, we're covered." It was one of his favorite sayings. It usually didn't bring me much comfort because I never much considered myself a "child," even a few years ago when I was one.

"Yeah, but I'm 13 now, so I guess I have to become a fool or something."

"You're still a child . . my child anyway. Just stay safe. Your mother and I worry about you every day with this Iraq thing going on.".

"Dad, don't worry about it. Iraq knows it would lose in a war with Israel. Nobody picks a fight they're sure to lose. People pick fights they think they'll win."

"I hope you're right."

The conversation ended on an up note. I went to my dorm room with my head swimming. Collins Christian Academy . . . it wasn't D'var Adonai, but right now that didn't matter. The way I'd heard Zippy talking, I wasn't sure I wanted to go to school with her any more. There had to be some other explanation. There just HAD to be. The idea that Zippy could just be using me made me feel like I was going to throw-up. And if it was true, what did that say about the other M-Gangers? Could Sivan REALLY have been trying to protect me? I'm glad Danny was off making out with Sherri somewhere. I wouldn't want him or anyone else to see me crying myself to sleep. I was so confused.

I had that nightmare again. Only this time, the bad guy was Shamil Hassan himself, and when I took his hand, he dropped the gun. I looked around, and Adara was there. She had grabbed Zippy by the hair just like she'd done to me. She slit Zippy's throat. I just stood there watching her gurgling and writhing, with eyes that looked back at me with horror and disgust. I woke up panting and sweating.

What the hell was wrong with me?

CHAPTER NINETEEN – OUT WITH IT

True to their word, we all got the week off after the Salimah mission. We did our usual Krav training, weapons training, third party protection training, and we studied missions that had been carried out by Mossad, IDF, and Shabak in the past . . . but my heart really wasn't in it. Every time we'd get started, my mind would wander off to the two scenarios playing out in my head - either Zippy has been lying and was using me, or I was a real jerk for not trusting her after all she'd done for me. Neither prospect really appealed to me.

After that week, we were all called into a special meeting with Sarah. Shabak intelligence said that one of Hassan's top remaining lieutenants had entered Tel Aviv to try and pick up the pieces after we'd neutralized two of his main players. Apparently Ms. Salimah had been working on something big when Zippy splattered her brains across the wall.

"Here is the target." Sarah sounded SO official and serious when she said it. "His name is Kamal Bashir. He was an up and coming lieutenant in Hassan's organization. He's in Tel Aviv for a meeting with several cells for something big. We just don't know what . . . and we don't care. If we stop him, we stop whatever it is. While we don't have any intel from our usual channels, four informants have each approached us with the same story in the last week. We'd normally never go forward like this, but we've got M-Gang, and you've already trained for a mission just like the one we're about to attempt."

We all looked around at each other. Each of us had only personally trained for two missions, and the last one was a disaster.

"We're going to copy the Nasser mission, only now Amir and Aaron get to be Alephs. Rachael and Danny will double Tsipporah and Mark as alternate Beits on opposite ends of the square."

There was one glaring question, though - in the Nasser mission, there were snipers to take out the bodyguards. I asked Sarah about this. Her response was "Well, IDF was a long time ago for me, but I'm going to take the sniper spot. I used to be a sharpshooter. I'm on this mission. The only actual Shabak agents on the ground will be the ones driving the getaway car."

This was incredible. We thought they'd never trust us to do our own mission again after the Salimah fiasco. Here they were a week later sending us out on our own again. I guess that part about only judging a mission by its result is more than just talk.

Monday, August 20, 1990

I woke up on the day of the mission still feeling wrong. I actually wasn't limping today. My privates were still sore, but not hurting constantly anymore. I dressed myself up in the exact same clownish tourist getup I wore for the Nasser mission. It had worked for that one. Why not do it again? Zippy also wore her ridiculous costume from that same mission. She smiled when she saw me. "Have your wax this time?"

She seemed to genuinely care about me. And she'd smiled every time she'd seen me this week. WHY? I hated not knowing. I REALLY hated it. When I saw her face beaming at me, I made myself a promise: I WOULD ask her about what I'd heard, as soon as we were safe back in Dallas. I wouldn't do it here in Israel, but I would ask her. I owed her that much.

When we all loaded into the car, there didn't seem to be any tension at all in the group. Amir and Aaron were actually eager. They each had stun-guns in their jackets, and were ready to zap Bashir into next week.

I didn't even feel nervous. We were to walk in, come out, give the signal, and walk away. It almost felt like a chore. I honestly just wanted to go back and relax by the pool. But that wouldn't occur for a couple of hours. We'd have to sit at an outdoor table playing cards for a couple of hours waiting for the whole thing to get into place. Of course, Sarah had warned us that secret operations are mostly waiting. Zippy had said it a few times as well. You wait and wait and wait and wait and wait, then after waiting a bit longer, the whole thing goes down in two very intense minutes. Then you spend a week decompressing.

The drive out wasn't anything like our previous missions. Where we'd previously ridden to our drop off points in complete silence, with everyone scared to death. This time everyone was laughing and having a great time. It was almost like a family outing. It felt more like we were heading to a picnic, rather than a counter-terror mission.

Sheri and Danny got dropped off first. Then about five minutes later, Zippy and I jumped out. I did the best to conceal the stabbing pain in my privates when I jumped out of the car. I guess I hadn't healed as much as everyone else thought, but I'd never let it show. We walked towards our surveillance spot without saying a word.

We sat down at the outdoor cafe across the street from

the hotel where Bashir was staying, and both bought these fruit drinks that I can't quite describe. Zippy pulled a deck of cards out of her jacket pocket and started shuffling. We'd already agreed to start with Baccarat, then move to seven card poker.

We played a few rounds in complete silence before our coms crackled. "This is Sarah. Katzav and I are in position. We've signaled Shabak to send the getaway car. When they signal that they're in place, we'll get started. It should only be about 45 minutes now, guys."

"Copy that." Zippy said it almost like she was reading a poem. She looked down at the cards. "Mark, is there something you need to tell me?"

That came out of nowhere.

I shook my head and shrugged my shoulders like I had no idea what she was talking about.

She kept looking down, "You've been off since the Adara mission. What's wrong?"

Great question Zipps. There's not a chance in hell I'm going to answer it, but you get points for perception. I'm confused. That's what's wrong. I KNOW I heard you essentially telling Sarah that you were using me. On the other hand, I KNOW that you really care about me. The two don't mix . . . of course, this all sounded horrible in my head. It wasn't going to come out of my mouth. The only thing that would come out was . . . "Nothing."

"Out with it, Mark. You can't keep stuff from me. You ought to know this by now. Are you . . . hurt or something. I know it's hard for boys to talk about but you can tell to me. Are you . . .." She leaned in to whisper to me. "Are you peeing blood?"

"I'm not injured."

"Then what's bothering you?"

What WASN'T bothering me? My parents wouldn't send me to D'var Adonai cause they were hung up about it being a Jewish school. My options were to go to this

Baptist school in Addison, or go back to Anderson and face that nightmare again. My closest friend in the world could be using me, or I could just be a horrible person for not trusting her. I tried to look away from Zippy's face. I looked over at a group of little kids. A couple of them were staring at us. That was odd.

"Look at me, Mark!" She wasn't going to let this go.

I sighed, looked back at her, thought for a few seconds to get the words right. "A few days ago I overheard a conversation with you and Sarah."

Zippy pursed her lips and looked like I'd just annoyed her. At great risk of life and limb, I continued, "I didn't get what you meant, but it sounded like you only wanted me here in M-Gang because I fit some kind of profile."

I looked away from her. Something wasn't right. As I looked around, a LOT of little kids were staring at us. This whole thing felt off.

"Mark . . you should have asked me this days ago. You've been wondering if I'd been lying to you? Using you? Mark, look at me!"

"Zippy, something's wrong."

"Yes. If there's anything you should never do, it's doubt me. I will never hurt you or lie to-"

"No. Zippy. Something's wrong here. Look around!!!"

She blinked and scanned the entire area. "Oh my goodness. We're being stared at from every direction. Are your weapons secure?"

I felt behind me. The gun wasn't showing. I just looked like a tourist. None of her weapons were showing either.

Zippy hit her coms button, "Aaron come in. I think we have a problem."

The coms crackled. It was Sheri. "We're aborting. Cohen, Dagan, get out of there. Everyone else, hold positions till they're away. Then walk away slowly and calmly."

What????

"Got it. Let's go." Zippy didn't hesitate. We both got up and started to walk away as calmly and normally as possible.

"Move it guys!!! You've been spotted by someone. They're coming for you - RUN!!!"

Ok, this one wasn't supposed to get physical. Now I was annoyed. We bolted down the street as fast as our legs would take us. I looked back to see a whole crowd of people - men, women, kids, all chasing us. The kids were picking up rocks and throwing them, but couldn't quite reach us with them yet. As we ran, I felt a stinging in my chest. The scab where Adara sliced me had rubbed open. Not good.

"Where's the car??" Sheri shouted into the coms. We kept running for a few seconds, BAM!!! A rock caught me in the shoulder-blade. I didn't even look back - no sense making my face a target. Just keep running!!!!! The coms crackled "Guys, the car is in the wrong area, you've got to get off that street yourselves."

The rocks started hitting me . . it was only a few more seconds before I was bound to stumble. Zippy shouted "Clear out, we'll take care of ourselves and check back in when it's safe." Nice - this from the girl who was eight feet ahead of me and not getting hit with small stones.

Several small rocks pelted me in the head, and one big one caught me right in the thigh. I went tumbling and the barrage of rocks started pummeling me. The crowd was running right at me.

One particularly large man was running right at me with what appeared to be a football sized chunk of concrete that he was about to launch at my face when BANG. His body crumpled to the ground. BANG BANG BANG BANG. There was a loud swell of screaming from the crowd. Zippy had shot four of the adults. Their bodies had fallen into the mass of children running at me. Most of the crowd turned and ran in terror. These folks were used to throwing rocks at soldiers who wouldn't shoot back . . or would at least fire warning shots. Zippy was playing for keeps.

She ran right at me. BANG BANG She killed two more. I knew she'd never shoot a child, but she'd have no problem sending every adult in that crowd to the grave. By the time she got to me, the rocks had stopped hitting me. "MOVE IT Cohen!!!!" She pulled me up by one arm and we kept running. A sharp, stabbing pain was shooting up my leg. The moment we turned our backs, several people started chasing after us with rocks. Some were even children. "Cohen, you will need to take out adults. Let me worry about the younger ones." She couldn't be serious!!!!! "NOW!!!"

I spun around, pulled my Beretta, and aimed center mass at the nearest adult. Click, Click, Click. Nothing happened. I was in trouble. Zippy looked straight into the eyes of the nearest child, and shot the ground right in front of his feet. It did the trick. The entire crowd went running. Those kids may have been used to throwing rocks at Israelis, but they weren't used to getting shot at. She emptied her clip, taking out a couple of the remaining adults. We turned and ran into the nearest alleyway. We made it all the way to the end before hearing a dreadful buzzing sound.

As I turned, I saw a motorcycle blazing towards us. The rider was holding a chain with one hand. BANG. Zippy had reloaded her gun and shot him before I even saw his face. The bike tipped over and skidded towards us at an off angle for a second before banging into the wall. The rider went skidding as well. But he never got back up.

I got my gun un-jammed, then turned to Zippy, "Looks like we have transportation. You drive, I'll shoot."

"No way, Cohen. You've never fired FROM a moving target before. I'm not putting my life in the hands of your aim."

I didn't argue. We both struggled for a second to get the

bike standing up again. Motorcycles are heavy!!! It took a few attempts to start before I got the engine going. Apparently, the poor motorcycle didn't like being turned over on its side. I got it just in time. I heard Arabic shouting at the end of the alleyway. We sped out, and I heard a few last BANG BANG noises from behind me.

"I'm out!!!!!!" Zippy grabbed the back of my shirt, and yanked the Beretta out of the back of my pants. I got the bike into 4th gear in no time, and we were blazing around 80 miles an hour. She didn't fire. I guess we got out okay. As we reached the end of the road, I tried to slow the bike as quickly as I could for the turn ahead, but it started shaking as I hit the brakes, like it was going to tip over. So I kept having to let off the brakes. I took the turn a lot faster than I should have. I didn't tip us far enough over into the turn, so it felt like we were going to go flying off the bike . . . and I made the fatal error of hitting the brakes in the middle of the turn. The bike went skidding on its side . . . on top of me. Zippy launched herself from it with her feet just before it hit the ground, and she went into a martial arts roll.

I laid on the ground for a few seconds, completely disoriented. She ran over to me. "Mark, we're not out yet. You've gotta keep moving!!!!"

My knee was all skinned, and my hip hurt like hell, but I did a limping run. I'd hate to think of how horribly comical I looked hobbling at top speed with Zippy pulling me by the hand as quickly as she could. She could have let go and sprinted off at any moment, but she didn't. She slowed herself down to keep me safe. This didn't seem like the behavior of someone using me as a disposable shield.

"Mark, you suck at the motorcycle!!!! I'll shoot myself before riding with you again." She was obviously annoyed. We went as fast as we could for about 15 minutes, till we were back on a familiar street where we both felt safe. Then we slowed to a walk. After a few more blocks, we stopped on a street corner and did some self-checking. Our coms were both broken during the rock throwing mess. Neither of us had any change so we couldn't use a pay phone to call M-Gang and tell them where to pick us up. So we were in for a long walk.

My hip was starting to turn black where I'd hit the ground in the motorcycle crash, and I was starting to shiver - first sign of shock. This wasn't good. We both started walking towards the center of Tel Aviv. There were several cafes around Dizengoff where we could order drinks and get change.

It was the opposite of our trip TO the mission. We had been all laughs then. Now we were completely silent. It was probably better that way. I was a little scared of finishing the conversation we'd began just before the mission went wrong.

CHAPTER TWENTY – CARDS ON THE TABLE

When you're being hyper-vigilant with a mix of exhaustion and the beginnings of shock, the oddest things jump out at you. The last half hour of our walk towards Dizengoff was an endless series of mental snapshots. There was the homeless guy laying on the street. I watched him nonstop. I knew he wasn't dead, but sleeping. He was likely either drunk or on drugs, lying in a puddle of his own piss. Yet I watched him as though he would spring up and start running at us. I kept imagining him as some secret agent working for Shamil Hassan. I kept my hand on my backup folding knife, watching him nonstop till he was no longer in sight.

Zippy and I walked next to each other in perfect sync - almost like soldiers . . . ragged, worn-out soldiers, but soldiers nonetheless. I wasn't even looking forward. I was looking at the ground. The sun was too bright, so my eyes were half closed anyway.

We crossed a street, and I saw a baby's pacifier just lying in the dirt on the side of the curb. I wondered what became of its owner. In all likelihood, the kid just spit it out and the mother was too busy to notice. She probably figured it out several blocks later, or when they got home, or maybe she still hadn't. Or maybe the kid had been kidnapped. Maybe the baby was dead. Maybe the mother beat the baby in a fit of rage, and realized only too late that she had killed her child. My mind was wandering off to some rather horrible scenarios. Maybe that was just the after effect of having a bunch of people try to kill me. Maybe I got some kind of damage from one of those rocks that hit me in the head.

Or maybe I was just an evil person at heart. Maybe I was the type of person who'd watch a bomb go off, killing dozens of people, just for the entertainment that a big bang would provide - like fireworks. Maybe hell was meant for people like me: the type of guy who'd trick his own grandma into taking a sip of vodka, just to get a good laugh from seeing her spit it across the kitchen. Maybe I was the type of coward to let a good person like Zippy take a bullet for me, and do nothing. Maybe the judging eyes I saw in my dream were more than just my mind tormenting me. Maybe it was my conscience . . if I even had one. How could I know?

"WAKE UP, Mark!!!!! Keep moving." Zippy had gone twenty feet ahead of me, and I was just standing there, staring at this baby's pacifier in the dirt. We had to get out of the sun.

We made our way to the busy streets of central Tel Aviv, and our old haunt - Dizengoff Mall. I'd imagined it would be much more of a relief than this, but I was so hot, and drenched in sweat. My clothes were sticking to my skin so tightly that I was starting to feel claustrophobic in my shirt and pants. I felt like I was going to suffocate if I didn't strip all my clothes off.

It was already evening when we got to the little cafe where we were going to calmly buy a few drinks to break our money into change, and make our phone call to M-Gang, requesting an extraction. It was an indoor cafe, much unlike the outdoor one where our disastrous adventure began a few hours earlier. My knife-wound was irritated as hell, my skinned up knee still burned, and my hip had turned completely jet black. I wasn't going to be able to hide this. When Zippy and I went through the automatically opening door, the rush of cold air immediately jolted me.

Some of the diners stared at us when we walked in. We'd obviously been through hell. We weren't your usual "night on the town" customers. We took our seats at the cafe, and Zippy ordered the exact same fruit drinks we'd had before everything went wrong a few hours earlier. I couldn't help but appreciate the irony. Here we were . . . again . . . at a cafe (albeit indoors), having these same fruit drinks . . . again, because this worked out so well for us last time, right?

Zippy chugged about half of hers. I started feeling good again after the first sip of mine. I don't know what all was in this drink, but it woke me out of my trance, or whatever it was.

"We need to get a doctor to look at your hip, and one of the lumps on your head which is starting to look egg sized." She sounded like my mom.

"No. I'm fine."

"Says the guy who no has seen what you look like at the moment. You no fine, Mark. You didn't get killed. Neither did I. That's about it."

I seriously wanted to keep the subject off my health, so I followed her thought. "How the hell did they spot us? Was it a trap all along? Did someone see one of our weapons? Did someone spot our teams on the roof? What happened."

Zippy sat for a few seconds before sighing and admitting what had been worrying her this entire summer.

"Last year when I supported Shabak on several missions, I always seen by people in the neighborhood. As a Beit, it was my job to be seen. I would distract, no? Anyway, it became the talk of the town. Whenever Shabak or Matkal going to raid a building, and someone get killed, there would to be this little girl somewhere nearby. They started calling me 'Angel of Death.' You remember Sarah talking about this. I've been afraid all summer long that on one of these missions, someone would spot me as that 'angel,' and compromise the mission. I am terrified that it happen today."

She huffed. "It would be worse for Israel if it was a trap. That would mean either informants were compromised, or they betrayed us in large numbers. But honestly, I more comfortable with that than thinking I compromised the mission just by being there . . . that I would compromise ANY mission by being there, because so many people seen me." She finished her drink.

"Zippy, if you've got a reputation, that means you're doing good. And there'll always be good for you to do. If you can't be a Beit anymore, fine. You can move on to Aleph and let someone else worry about being a distraction."

"This did no work so well either, no?"

"Well, you DID take out Adara Salimah. And you took out that Savak team when you were a kid." Oh crap!!! I'd done it now. I wasn't ever supposed to mention that . . as evidenced by the sudden look of annoyance on her face. Why can't I keep my big mouth shut?

"Mark. I want to protect people. That sometimes mean I harm evil people. I do neither if I can no be invisible. I no want to be a legendary assassin. I want to be an invisible force for good."

"But you ARE legendary."

She just shook her head. "You can have the legend. Any of the M-Gangers can have it. I no care. I would to be happier. I'm happy about the lives I've saved. Everyone I ever killed has been bad, and would have hurt and killed innocent people if I no had done what I did. I think about the lives saved. I no want 'Legend of Tsipporah: Teenage Angel of Death.' I am no bringer of death." She took another sip of her drink. "I am protector of life. I just have to use death to do it. In fact, . . ." She grabbed the symbol on her necklace - the Star of David with the weird writing on it. ". . . that's what this symbol means. This writing says 'khai' which is Hebrew for 'Life.' It is symbol of life having victory over death. I am protector of life - like doctor."

She counted the change from her order. "Speaking of doctor, we need to get you to one. We have enough to use a pay phone. I will to call Sarah and they send a car to come get us."

I didn't care so much for this idea. "Can't we wait here a while?"

"Mark, you do need doctor - and sooner is better than later."

"I know but . . . she was going to kick me out after Adara. When she sees me like this, I'm finished."

She gave me a confused look. "Mark, why would you ever think Sarah want you out of M-Gang? Were you no listening at my door a few days ago? Did you no hear?"

"It sounded like she wanted to throw me out. And everyone was hiding something from me. I can put two and two together."

She smiled a bit. "But you can no put two and three together when you only see two and two."

It took me a second or two to process that. "So what was all that? Sivan trying to protect me from you? You telling Sarah you were using me? Sarah saying that was the only reason she'd let me stay?"

She suddenly leaned forward, and whispered intensely, "Sarah was trying to protect you. So was I. So was Sivan. We no wanted you to know because we no wanted you to

WORRY. You been through so much, we no wanted to add this worry."

"Worry about what? What was Sarah protecting me from?

She sighed again. "First, I call Sarah. We need to get you to a doctor. I answer you when I get back." She got up to go make the call.

When she got back, she continued, "Some of the people in charge over Sarah . . over my mom and dad. They no think you should be in the program. They no like idea of non-Jew in Jewish program. The Adara thing gave them excuse they were looking for. After you nearly get killed, they try to have you removed and sent home to America immediately. They pretend to be worried about your safety. They took things Sivan had said last month when she was mad at me, and put them together with the Adara thing, and make their case."

"What did Sivan tell them last month?"

Zippy's hesitation to answer really built up my worry. "She was worried about me. She noticed that I act differently with you. She know my real reasons for recruiting you."

Oh no!!! I wasn't sure I wanted to hear the next part.

"She know how important you are to me - how much I want to protect you from the darkness. She thought I was obsessing over you. Is just . . . you really important to me."

"But why? Why me? There are hundreds of kids bullied in schools and stuff. Why did you pick me?"

She seemed to wait forever before answering again - just staring down at the table. "I no ready to say. Please just trust me. I no using you. Is just very important to me that you be safe from darkness."

That was good enough for me. I'd been waiting to hear this. I'd been dying for some sign that she really was being honest with me all this time, and that the things she told Sarah were all made up. I looked at her, and this thing inside of me was screaming at me to say "I love you." All I had to do was muster up the guts. I took a deep breath, and was just about to blurt it out, when she continued.

"Sarah ask me to give reason for why you should be a member - logically, without my personal feelings. When one of them talk to Sivan last month, she say that I had this personal thing for you, and that this was the only reason you were in the program. I had to be able to give her better reason. I had to say you no just belong here because I want you here. You no just belong here because we are your friends, and all of us . . . even Sivan . . . we all want you here. I gave reason that you belong here because you are the casting mold for the type of person they want to recruit, and they need to watch you over the next several years."

I was so disappointed in myself. I should have trusted her.

"Mark, those things I told Sarah - they basically bought you a lifetime membership in M-Gang without review. And when they re-interview Sivan about you yesterday, she said same thing. You in for good because of what we say. But please never think we using you or only-"

BANG!!!!!!!!! There was a HUGE explosion right outside the cafe. All the windows blew out. Zippy and I both ducked under the table. Someone had set off a car bomb. I looked up, half dazed, and saw some men in black walking a little too calmly towards the café – towards US!!!!!!

CHAPTER TWENTY-ONE – A DEAL WITH THE DEVIL

Absolute panic ensued. People were madly scrambling from the cafe. Once we got a grip on ourselves and put a lid on the instinctual desire to go running and screaming like everyone else, Zippy and I got up and started looking for anyone who was too calm.

We didn't need to look too hard. All the calm faces were working their way through the fleeing masses of people . . . right towards us. I counted 5 of them, but I knew there were more. Before I could say anything, Zippy had already engaged one that I hadn't even seen. She'd doubled him over with one groin shot, forward-elbowed his throat as he was going down, and kneed him in the face. Blood splattered everywhere. His face had exploded on her knee. His body slumped to the ground. Another one pulled a gun on her, but she'd already grabbed it by the barrel. BANG!!!! It fired right into the man she'd just put on the ground. She launched in, two hands on the gun.

I couldn't watch, though. The five I'd originally counted were now charging towards us: one for Zippy and four for me. Maybe they thought the girl would be easier and only required one more guy. Boy did they misjudge!!!!

Of course, this was REALLY bad for ME. I couldn't take on four trained bad guys. The best I could do would be to not get killed, knocked out, or dragged off before she could finish her last two bad guys and come over to save me. So of course, my first move was to pick up a chair and throw it at them before they could get near me. It bought me a second or two, so I picked up another one.

BANG, BANG, BANG, CLICK!!!! Zippy had wrestled the gun from her assailant, and emptied it into him. In a flash she turned and threw it right at the face of the other terrorist who was running towards her. She charged in on him.

I threw the second chair at the one closest to me. He deflected it, only stopping for a second. Another one ran past him and grabbed me by the shirt. I threw a kick right into his groin and reached across my chest for his wrist. The kick didn't seem to really hurt him, but his body did flinch just barely enough for me to get him into the wrist lock. It was the exact same move Zippy had done to Mr. Peters a few months ago, and it ACTUALLY WORKED. I threw him to the ground face first - a full grown adult!!! But before I could do anything else, I felt an arm wrap completely around my throat and pull me back into a VIOLENT headlock. I'd stopped one bad guy, but I'd messed up and turned my back on three others.

As he spun me around, I saw Zippy - she had her attacker's shoulder locked, and he was doubling over under a barrage of her signature groin kicks. She slid her hand down the side of his face, grabbing his chin. CRACK!!!! She snapped his neck. He slumped dead to the ground.

I tried the move she'd taught me for getting out of a headlock. It completely failed. I couldn't move the arm that was locked around my throat like a steel vice, so I did the next best thing - slap to the groin from behind, then reach both hands over my right shoulder and claw at the face!! The groin shot did nothing, but I think one of my fingers jammed into an eye when I clawed at his face. That loosened him up, and when I did the "get out of a headlock" move again, his arm budged. I pivoted violently, ramming my shoulder into his body, and scooted out to the rear as quickly as I could. But two other guys were immediately on top of me.

I was running out of steam. I was so dizzy that the entire room was spinning in circles. I couldn't breathe.

I punched one of them in the throat, and tried to lock up on him, but the other one tackled me into the wall, spinning me into a half-nelson. The one I'd just throat-punched fell to his knees grabbing at his throat. I'd punctured his trachea. He was going to die. The guy who'd headlocked me a few moments ago pulled out a knife and lunged at me. There was nothing I could do - I was dead.

Zippy suddenly appeared behind him, reached around his face, grabbed his chin, and CRACK!!! She'd snapped his neck before he even knew she was there. Angel of Death indeed!!!! The guy who was holding me threw me into the wall and went for Zippy. Her right hand shot into his face at blur speed, her left shot to the side of it nearly as fast. CRACK!! She'd managed her third neck-snap of this encounter.

The last terrorist, the one I'd thrown into the wall, was getting up to his feet. I think we both wanted to let him go, but at the same time we both saw him make a run for the gun one of his friends had dropped. She charged towards him. He got to the gun and picked it up just in time for Zippy to get to him. With one hand on his elbow and the other on the weapon, she turned it inward on him. BANG!!!!

He'd shot himself. Zippy tore the gun from his hands, and backed away as quickly as she could while he fell to the floor.

BANG, BANG, BANG, BANG, CLICK!!! She emptied the gun into him.

We were both panting at this point, trying to catch our breath. I went over to check on the guy I'd hit in the throat. He was convulsing. Even if I'd wanted to save him, I didn't know how to do a tracheotomy. I couldn't have done a thing, so I just watched him. I also recognized him - it was Bashir. Our target had managed to find us, for all the good it did him. After a few moments, there were 7 dead bodies lying around us. I did a quick self-check, just like they'd taught me. Nothing bleeding. Nothing hurting too much. My head was clear.

"Zippy?"

"I'm ok, Mark."

"Let's get the hell out of here!!!!!"

"We can't, Mark,"

Her voice was a little too calm. Something was wrong. Before I could turn around, I heard him. The voice was a little high-pitched for a man. I turned around to face him, but knew who he was even before focusing my eyes on his face.

"So you're the Angel of Death" he mused. It was Hassan!!! It was Hassan himself!!!!! He was smirking. He was also aiming a 9 millimeter right at my face. I'd once heard a cop say that any gun being pointed at you looks huge, even if it's an itty-bitty little .22 like mine. He was right. It doesn't matter how big a gun is or isn't. When you're staring down the barrel, it looks like a cannon!!!

Hassan wasn't even looking at me. He was speaking to Zippy while keeping his gun on me.

"And this boy must be your sidekick. Well . . . this is a shock in so many ways. We all thought the 'Angel of Death' was an IDF Special Forces soldier dressed like a little girl. But I guess appearances aren't always so deceiving, are they. Nobody would expect the Zionists to use a real child . . . I guess there is no limit to their depravity."

Zippy spat out something in another language at him. I have no idea what it was, but one need not speak a language to know that it wasn't polite. Yet he only laughed.

"I'm the bad guy here? I'm just a man fighting for his people. You're the ones doing the killing, or have you had a look around here, little girl."

"They tried to kidnap us!" Sheesh, did I say that? My better sense was telling me to SHUT UP and not provoke him. But oddly enough, he lowered his gun, and studied me with his eyes for a few seconds.

"You're American. I studied in America." He paused for a second, glanced over at Zippy, then looked directly back at me, as though he was searching my face for a secret, "She must be some con artist to trick you into coming here to die for her and her people."

"You're wrong. Zippy's my friend."

"Zippy. As in Tsipporah Dagan??? From Texas?"

He looked at her for a second.

"Well, the surprises keep coming don't they. So you're the little bitch who killed my entire US team!!!!"

She was looking at him with raging hatred.

"And yet you seem so small. How's your friend Ms. Katzav???"

She spat out some more foreign profanities at him, but he only laughed.

"I guess I shouldn't take that too personally. After all, you've already killed the men who went after her family."

Did I hear that right? The guys Zippy killed also went after Sivan's family?

"But now you've apparently started recruiting . . ."

He looked at me for what seemed like forever.

"Ms. Dagan here brought you into this mess. She risked YOUR life because you're nothing to them. They only care about Jewish blood, and you're not Jewish are you?"

How did he know that? My name is Jewish. My

features are Jewish. How did he know?

"What's your name, son?"

"Mark."

"Are you Jewish, Mark?"

I shook my head. "Catholic."

"Ah, that's what I thought. Not so Jewish as the ones who are safely back at Mossad's headquarters or wherever your little team is staying, huh." He paused again, studying my face. What was he looking for? "Listen Mark, she's using you. You're nothing to her. She was probably watching you for years, waiting for the right moment to lure you in. And now here you are ready to take a bullet for her."

Zippy yelled, "Mark, that's not tr-"

"SHUT UP, JEW!!!!!!!!!" he screamed, violently pointing the gun at her. I actually saw her flinch for a moment, but she recomposed herself quickly. So did he, lowering the gun again.

He studied me for a few seconds. The look on his face turned to one of bewilderment, "Are you the son of Richard and Jennifer Cohen?"

How the hell did he know that?

"I see you are."

I really need to work on my poker face. He's a little too good at reading people.

"I'd bet you don't even know why the Dagan's moved to Dallas. You don't even know the role your idiot parents played in all this. You don't know why Tsipporah targeted you. And now you're fighting for her . . killing for her, even. She'll have you doing all of her dirty-work before long. She'll send you to do the dangerous work that they won't have Jews doing. She'll have you taking all the risks. And if you get killed, she and her friends will just pick up some other . . formerly Jewish goy . . to replace you. She'll tell him all the same sweet things she whispered to you. She'll make him feel loved for the first time in his life, and he'll be the next one standing here, thousands of miles from his home, his mom, his dad, his family . . his whole world, about to die. I've been keeping tabs on her since she killed my US team four years ago. Trust me, son. You're nothing to them."

"Mark?" Zippy actually sounded scared, like she could see his words affecting me. It sounded crazy, but it also sounded like it . . . could be true. Could Zippy have been using me after all? Did it even matter anymore? We were going to die.

"She'll steal your very life."

"Mark, it's not true!!!!"

I was frozen with fear. I felt my jaw shaking. I felt a tear run down my cheek. Damn!!!!! I was crying in front of an international terrorist. Local kid from Plano stares down international terrorist, and bravely . . . breaks down and cries.

"Listen, I don't want to hurt you." His voice softened. "You don't have to die here. We want to be your friends - especially considering who your father is. We are the ones who want peace, not these . . . leaches who are sucking your life away. Come with me. I promise nobody will hurt you. My people will get you safely back to your home." He held out his hand. HE HELD OUT HIS HAND. The gun was still in his right, but his left was reaching out to me . . . with a face that honestly said friendship.

I kept seeing that scene from Fright Night. Jerry Dandridge was holding out his claw of a hand. "Take my hand, Edward." God, I was so scared. I'd seen this in my dreams.

"Mark! Don't listen to him!! He's Savak!! He's lying. He's going to kill us. Mark, for God's sake!!!!!!"

I saw "Evil Ed" and I saw Zippy and all the times she'd stood up for me, and I heard her crying "I love you" back at the hotel after the Adara fiasco. I saw my dream - I knew how this would end. And I thought of my family, who I may never see again. I saw my sister's face - I loved the kid so much. Evil Ed was shaking as he reached towards the claw that was extended to him. I just wanted to go home. I didn't even realize I'd been walking towards him.

"Come with me son. Let me show you that we are the ones who want peace."

I closed my eyes and cleared my head. After a few seconds, I opened my eyes and said, "Nice try, but you've got the wrong Cohen. That might have worked on my parents, but I ACTUALLY KNOW THE DIFFERENCE between those who want to kill me, and those who'd lay down their lives to protect me!!!"

Oh boy I'd done it now. I knew I was going to die. It's a strange feeling to know that and actually not be afraid anymore. You think of the strangest things. For some reason, I wanted to utter some final words that would make my friends and family proud. When all hope is gone, all you have left is who and what you are.

"We have a saying in Texas: 'Remember the Alamo.' It means the same thing to us as 'Never Again' means to Israel. Do those two words sound familiar, you worthless Savaki trash?"

. . . and while I knew it was ME that was saying it, I swear it sounded like Zippy. But she wasn't saying anything. She was just watching. The teacher, bursting inside with pride as her student stood up to be counted with millions of brave good guys who held their ground even unto death.

It was Hadassah standing up to Haman . . . or in this case Hassan.

His face was completely crestfallen. "You disappoint me . . . Texan" He spat the word out with the same venomous hatred that he'd said the word "Jew" with earlier. He shook his head and pointed his gun directly at Zippy's face.

"Allah Akbar" he muttered. I heard Zippy behind me

whisper "Shema Israel . ."

I didn't think. My body just moved without me: burst forward, open close, right hand on the trigger guard, left on his forearm, both thumbs to the sky, push pull, side head-butt, break and take, tap and rack. I'd disarmed him, and didn't even realize it. I was shielding Zippy with my entire body, and pointing the gun center mass on him.

"Akbar this!"

I don't even remember pulling the trigger, just feeling the gun jumping in my hands again and again and again until it was only clicking. I remember dropping it and falling to my knees.

I remember Zippy putting her arms around me.

I remember sirens.

I remember the Shabak guys all patting me on the back and telling me how I ought to come join them some day. The black-cards were doing the same.

I remember a bunch of Hebrew chatter that I had no hope whatsoever of understanding. Zippy said I'd screamed like a banshee when I burst in on Hassan, but I'll never admit remembering that detail.

The next few hours were a blur. We were taken to a hospital somewhere in Tel Aviv, then whisked back to our little dormitory near Wingate. It was there that Zippy put her arms around me and just said over and over "Todah. Todah, Mark. Todah."

I finally stopped her. "Why are you thanking me?

"You saved my life."

"You saved mine a couple of times. Hell, you ought to trade in 'Angel of Death' for 'Mark's Full Time Guardian Ange-"

"I EXPECT to save your life, Mark! You need someone to."

"Uh . . thanks." Of all the sarcastic things she'd ever said, that was probably the first time I'd felt truly insulted.

"I mean it. You are magnet for darkness and people

who want to hurt you. I expect to have to save you. But I'm the so called 'Angel of Death'. I should no expect to have my life saved - ever, especially by someone with so little training as you. Last spring, you could no even to protect yourself from your fellow middle-schoolers. How could I possibly expect you to save ME from someone like Hassan?"

"Yes, but the training I've had has been . . . "

"I know. But even that could no awaken the monster in you - that thing that let you stand up to Hassan. Techniques can be taught. Aggression can be taught. But bravery is either already there or it is no there."

"Zippy, that wasn't bravery. He was going to kill you and he expected me to just go along with him."

"I thought he was convincing you."

"Convincing me to betray the only true friend I've ever had?"

"But you learned of how I watched you before we recruited you. You knew that it was all planned."

"So?"

"You thought I'd lied to you."

"Again, so?"

"I no understand."

"Zippy, every friend I had turned their backs on me last spring. EVERY ONE of them." Oh boy, I felt the lump in my throat. I was going to cry again. This was becoming an embarrassing habit. "And just when everyone else was leaving me, you came along. You gave me my life back. And you've been the truest friend I've ever known. You've stuck by me when it was insanity to do so. And you've made me strong. You rescued me from that darkness."

Now she was beginning to cry.

"Mark, there is more to this than you know. I SO want to tell to you everything, Mark. I really do love you. I want to . . . I just . . . give to me time. I promise you to know everything soon." She kissed me on the forehead. "Thank you so much for believing in me."

We hugged . . . for hours. You'd think kids in our position would be making out. We were alone. We were together. We liked each other a lot. And we'd just had a BIG adventure. If the James Bond movies were to be believed, we should have been making out, but after everything, just holding on felt perfect.

CHAPTER TWENTY-TWO – AN ANGEL IS BORN

Wednesday, August 22, 1990

The rest of the M-Gang kids went home on their regularly scheduled flights, but Zippy and I had to spend an extra day answering questions. When two teenage kids wipe out a team of 7 Iranian agents who'd been working support for PLO terror attacks . . . let's just say there are folks in Israel who take notice of such things. So we ended up retelling the story of every single moment we'd spent in Israel about a dozen times over for different investigators from different agencies.

Of course, there was this one other little matter - the bit about us also taking out Hassan – one of the biggest terrorists in the region, a guy Mossad and Shabak had been wanting but couldn't seem to get their hands on for years. There was a lot of patting our backs.

Before the rest of the kids got in their vans to head to the airport, Sivan even gave me a hug and told me how awesome she thought I was. SIVAN no less!!! The girl who thought I was a waste of skin. When Sivan of all people thinks you're cool, you MUST be doing something right.

There were also a couple of guys from Sayeret Matkal congratulating me, and talking like Zippy and I would be honorary members for life. The highlight of the day came when we got to meet Director Shavit himself - the man in charge of Mossad, and the man who green-lit the entire M-Gang program. It was one of the best days ever!!!

At the end of the day, Director Shavit put us on his private 707. Zippy's parents and Avi all dozed off immediately. Of course, anybody who's ever flown TO America over the Atlantic knows that these flights usually take place during the daytime. And it's 3 PM for about 7 hours nonstop. Night-flights this direction are not so common. It was weird for midnight to last forever, but it was also kinda cool.

Zippy went up to nudge her parents awake for a minute or two and ask them a few questions, then she came back to our little semi-private area.

"So" she said with a bit of a playful grin "how was YOUR summer vacation?"

"Well, let's see, I stopped an international terrorist, got to watch my best friend take out a team of trained soldiers, I learned to ride a motorcycle, got to fly in an F-15, and got to go out for a night on the town with the coolest chick on the planet. Do you think that holds up to a few miserable days of standing in line for hours in the sun at Disney, and a few trips to an overcrowded swimming pool? Hmmm . . . I'll have to think about that one."

She was laughing. "Yeah. Never a dull moment for us M-Gangers. Of course, you still have to PRETEND that you enjoyed Disney. Remember which rides you liked best?"

"Space Thunder?"

"Space MOUNTAIN. Sheesh, you're going to get us

killed some day."

She was the old Zippy again - my friend from last summer, who kicked over the porta-potty. Of course, this moment didn't last long. Leave it to Zippy to turn all serious on me. "Listen, you probably only have a day or two till the nightmares start. When they do, please tell me. You should no have to this do alone."

"Nightmares?"

"Mark, you killed two people. Even in defense of self and friends, killing someone hurts you on the inside. It tears at you and haunts you. The first will be the nightmares."

"What, reliving the whole thing?"

"Sometimes. Sometimes you will dream that you did nothing and died, or got me killed. Sometimes you will just see the faces of the ones you killed, judging you, haunting you . . and sometimes coming after you. I've been through this. You no are alone. Please tell me when the nightmares start."

"I will. Sheesh. You had nightmares?? I thought you were . . ."

"Invincible? The tough chick that took out entire Savak team when I was nine years old?"

"Well . . . yeah."

Her eyes looked a little sad for a moment, then she looked down. She sighed. I didn't know if I should say something or not. She looked up, staring past me. She was clearly lost in the past.

"I heard a noise. I was in the bathroom, changing into my Shabbat dress when I heard it - a slight hissing sound. I had the morning off from school, and there was to be a ceremony at my school that afternoon. So I was going to be dressed for the occasion. My parents had left me home alone. I could do anything I want except swim alone . . ."

She let a small grin crack through the sadness.

". . . which is exactly what I doing for the last hour."

The grin slowly faded from her face. She looked off into the distance.

"The TV was on in the living room. It was playing Reading Rainbow . . 'butterfly in the sky, I can go twice as high' . . and a little kid was talking about book called 'A Story A Story.' I remember that for some reason. I can no tell why I remember that. I never remember anything from TV, but I remember that. But the noise I'd heard was no on the TV. It was the back door. For all their security paranoia, my parents never figured out that if you push it up at just the right angle, it will open even if locked."

A single tear streaked down her face.

"I was terrified. I heard voices speaking in Arabic, but I no understood what they were saying. We'd gone over it a thousand times - if anyone finds us this is what you to do, but I was frozen there in the bathroom, half dressed, hair still soaked. I ran to room of my parents, and grabbed my mom's Walther from her bedside - the same PPK I loaned to you."

She started quivering ever so slightly as she spoke.

"My hands would no work right. It was like a bad dream where you try to scream but no noise come. My hands just would no move right. I was shaking. My whole body was shivering like it was freezing, but it was warm. I put gun under the pillow, and racked it as slowly as I could to cover the noise, but I just could no stop shaking. I wanted to be brave. I wanted to run out into hall and shoot them all, but I was SOOOO scared."

Her voice started to crack. It didn't even look like Zippy anymore. This was a child speaking to me - like any child afraid of the dark, crying while telling you about the nightmare that scared them.

"I ran and hid in closet. All my hand-to-hand combat training, all my weapons training, all the tactics, the rehearsals . . and I was hiding, too terrified to move."

She paused for several seconds, then looked at me with

eyes barely containing the boiling rage within.

"The kids all tell stories of how 'awesome' Zippy is. 'She took out entire wet team at age nine.' I was hiding in the closet, crying, shaking, and unable to do anything because I was so terrified!!! There's awesome for you!!"

She was gritting her teeth now as she spoke. The disgust on her face was venomous. She looked like she was about to spit - like the most bitter taste in the world was in her mouth. And she was breathing heavily as though she was in physical pain. But after a few moments, she calmed back down and looked off into the distance again.

"I remember praying the Shema, because I thought I would to die. So I was whispering the Shema over and over and over, and they find me. There were four of them. The one who find me . . . he had this horrible grin on his face. He jerked me up off the floor by my left arm."

And with that, she fell back into the same unnatural calm I'd seen so many times. "My right arm put gun to his face and squeeze trigger. He never saw it coming."

She looked back at me again.

"I no remember much of what happened next. I know I shot two others, but I no think I ever even saw their faces. It was just 'red dot, center mass, crush grip, push/pull, squeeze.' But the last one . . . I see his face. He was panicking. He as scared as me. I watch him die, and as he die I watch him become frightened child. The look on his face begging for doctor, begging to save him, and begging me to stop squeezing trigger, begging to no let him die . . . begging to no MAKE him die. But I just kept squeezing trigger. I could no stop till gun was clicking. I still see that face in nightmares."

She was openly sobbing now.

"And now I am 'legend assassin' . . . whatever. There's nothing 'legendary' about killing someone, especially when they trying to hurt you. You just do what you have to do. But there even less legend when you stop them and you just keep shooting."

"Zipps, you were just a kid. You couldn't have-"

"YOU NO SEE HIM!!!!! I stop him. I shoot him in chest, he fell to knees and I just keep shooting. His face beg me to stop and I just keep shooting. I was so scared. I was just so scared . . . "

She turned to look out the window at the light on the end of the plane's wing. In the darkness, it was blinking on . . . off . . . on . . . off . . . on . . . off. We could have floated away on the overwhelming hum of the engine in the darkness.

"I stop shaking after a while. I felt numb all over. I closed bedroom door and reloaded my mom's gun. If there were others, they'd have to come in through door, and I'd have an easy center mass shot. I guess my training kicked in or something. I called my dad, and told him what happen. I called police. Then I wait in room with dead bodies. Police took pictures. They put chemical on my hands to see if I really shoot gun or not. They put up tape. They have counselor or somebody to talk to me. Then my dad show up. They quiz him. Then the NSA counter-terror team show up and sends everyone else home. It was all a blur. I could no stand to stay in house anymore, so when my parents were no looking, I walked out into the hot afternoon air, still wearing Shabbat dress, covered in blood."

She'd started breathing heavily again. It was condensing on the window in a pulsating pattern.

"I felt so dirty - so tainted. People had broken into my HOME, into my mother's room - the place I always felt the most safe. It was like a piece of my insides had been violated. I never feel safe anywhere ever again. And I kill someone - taken a life. I could never to take that back. I would always be someone who had killed. I felt . . . stained, like I never be clean again. So I just kept walking. I ended up at a creek, and I just walked . . . stumbled along."

She hesitated. Something was eating her up on the inside - something which was hurting her more than even the thought of killing, and she really didn't want to tell me.

"I walked until I found this tree. My head was burning from the sun, so I stop under the shade. I fell down to my knees in front of tree. I could no stand it anymore. I open my mouth and tried to scream, but only this horrible whining noise came out. I punched the tree, and finally a scream came out. I scream a few times, and just started crying uncontrollably. I felt like I would throw up. Nothing would ever be happy again. I killed four people - I could never be the happy little girl playing with her dolls or doing stupid fun things again. I could no stop seeing his begging face. I just could no get it out. I could never be free from that image IN MY HEAD!"

She accentuated each word with a hard knock on her forehead.

"I cried for long time and then for some reason, I just stopped. I felt nothing. I stood up and leaned on tree."

She looked at me with an intense focus. "I was lost in the darkness. A nearby school let out, and I was watching the children go play on the playground. I wanted to be them SOOOO badly. I wanted to know nothing about Savak. I wanted to take it all back and never know what it was like to be so afraid. But I could no even imagine what it would be like to play and be free of such things."

She paused for a few more seconds. There was a struggle going on in her heart. Even I could tell. What could possibly be eating her more than what she'd already told me.

"Then I saw this . . thing happening off in the distance. There was group of boys my age bullying some kid. I never seen something like that before, but they were pushing him around. It did no make sense. I kept thinking 'just HIT one of them' but he do nothing. I watched it with absolute horror. I just killed four trained adults. This little boy was getting beaten up by four other children and he could no make it stop. I heard the other boys giggling . . and I saw the horrible grin on the face of the man who jerked me up from my mother's closet. I wanted to run after them. I wanted to fight again!!!! I started feeling this rage boiling up in my chest. I was so angry."

She looked directly into my eyes, her face half angry, half offering an apology.

"Then one of the bullies shoved the little boy down into a mound of fire-ants."

WHAT?!?!?

She could see it on my face. "Yes. I was there that day. You screamed. You ran and jumped into creek. I saw the whole thing."

She was there?!?!? She was there the day those kids beat me up and pushed me into a fire ant mound four years ago??? I couldn't breathe. I still had a scar on my hand from the trip to the emergency room.

"I realized in that moment that there was a reason for me to go through what I went through. I had a purpose - it was to protect people. Evil would prey on those who can't fight. So I would fight it back and protect them. In that moment, only hours after getting lost into darkness, a light broke through. There was a purpose . . . a goal. I had to watch over people like this little boy."

I tried really hard to maintain my poker face. I couldn't let her see how shocked I was at hearing all this.

She continued, "I asked kids at my synagogue who the little boy that got shoved into the ant bed was. I learned all about you. When I heard you were attending the cotillion classes, I asked my parents to enroll me. It was no accident that we became friends there. I wanted to make sure nothing bad ever happen to you again. I wanted to be your guardian angel."

Guardian angel????

"Believe it or no, the boys tried to threaten me

afterward. But when I decide to fight him, they all ran."

Wow!!!!!

"Anyway, after a while, I genuinely began to feel like you were real friend. Last summer, when we were riding bikes all over town, we were real friends. That was one of the happiest times that I can remember in my life. I got to just be Tsipporah - normal girl, if only for a short while. That was also right after I got back from Israel, and my first meeting with Director Shavit. I was going to protect many people now . . . and I could just be friends . . . or maybe even girlfriend of the boy in my neighborhood."

She let out a slight giggle, which mixed with her tears to make her burning sadness show through.

"But I got so busy with training last fall . . . . "

She was getting distant again . . .

"I can no tell you how dark I felt the day Sheri tell me about the things that happen to you at school."

. . . and gritting her teeth again.

"I could protect you from darkness everywhere but in your school."

She sighed.

"Well . . . I found a way to protect you from the darkness anyway, no? I would train you to fight it yourself, and talk my parents into letting you join OUR fight. Give YOU a purpose. Give YOU the power to wield violence . . instead of always cowering when it approach you. Give YOU some of what I had."

And she smiled.

"So you see - you think I rescued you from the darkness, but you also rescued ME. You rescued me that day when I thought I was lost, when I was looking for why all these horrible things come into my life. When you suffered that day, it made me strong. Now I make you strong. We save each other."

She looked down, closed her eyes, and took a deep breath. After a moment, she opened them back up, and looked at me with a big smile on her face.

"Ok, enough sentimentality. Time for a movie."

Wow she shifts gears quickly - more than even me. I had to ask "a movie?"

"Yeah. Director Shavit's plane has a VCR, and I've been waiting all month to spring this on you."

"Spring what on me?" As though finding out that my best friend in the world had been both stalking me and acting as my guardian angel for years wasn't "springing something" on me.

"A gift. I bought this for you last month, but never could seem to find the right time to give it to you."

Okay, I was curious.

"After all the times we sat around the lounge at M-Gang Israel watching Charlie and Peter fighting off the evil Jerry Dandridge, I knew you would no be able to resist this."

She rummaged through her backpack, and pulled out a video tape - a gift she'd bought me during one of our many trips to Dizengoff Mall.

"Consider this Mossad's thank you for killing one of the biggest and scariest terrorists in the world, and saving their 'Angel of Death.'"

She smirked as she handed it to me. And yes, it was something I'd been dying to see. And yes, you better believe we spent the next hour and a half cuddled up in the back of the plane watching it. And yes, we did both make it to the end before dozing off and sleeping the rest of the longest night of our lives (literally) away.

Fright Night part 2!
Awesome!!!!!!!!!!!!!!!!!!!

CHAPTER TWENTY-THREE – MODEH ANI

We woke up a few hours before landing. It was morning. Zippy and I talked a bit over breakfast. I asked her what Hassan had meant about my mom and dad being involved. She didn't know the answer, but promised she'd ask her parents and get back with me.

When we landed, my parents and Elise were at the airport waiting. There were plenty of hugs and "tell me all about it" comments. I was pretty banged up, so I told them all about my newfound interest in "sports." I was enthusiastic enough that they bought it. They also noted how muscled up and tanned I'd gotten.

Zippy and I hugged goodbye, and I was off with my family. They asked if I was ready to start school next week. It didn't bother me at all. I was Mark Cohen - an agent in Mossad's youth team, the guy who took out Shamil Hassan, and helped take out two of his lieutenants. My best friend was Tsipporah L. "Zippy" Dagan, leader of Mossad's youth team. People were free to mess with me at their own TREMENDOUS peril. Not that I'd ever say this part to my parents, or anyone else for that matter . . . and that was going to be the hardest part. I'd done something of worldwide and historic importance, but I couldn't tell a soul. All would be fine as long as I didn't receive an international phone call from the Israeli Prime Minister to congratulate me.

We piled into my dad's big red Suburban. It was nearly 10 in the morning, but I was pretty well gone. You can sleep for a bit on a plane, but it's like you're not really asleep. You still end up exhausted. I was unconscious before we even got out of the airport.

Friday, August 24, 1990

I dressed up a bit more than anyone should in August, and my mom drove me to Collins Christian Academy. It was a white building attached to the side of a church. I went inside and found my way to the office. My mother drove off. She had errands to run.

Once in the office, I was greeted by a man in his mid-to-late 40s who identified himself as "Brother Michael." WOW that sounded weird. He was a soft spoken man, and had a gentle demeanor.

I distrusted him immediately.

He just struck me as the type to be all about the Bible and being good all day, but at night he's secretly having an affair with one of the kindergarten teachers. He was the principal at Collins, and he had to interview every single student before admission. I wasn't very nervous talking to him. I just had to be careful to not mention my tape collection, or the fact that I was going to a rock concert in about ten hours. I'd read in the school's application packet that this school forbad students from listening to any rock music. Apparently they thought that all popular music was somehow Satanic. Weird.

Brother Michael (I'd REALLY have to get used to

calling him that) gave me a quick orientation lecture on how this wasn't like a public school. Kids here are much better behaved, and behavior which may seem normal in a public school wouldn't be tolerated here. We'd see about that.

I had to take an "aptitude test" before final admittance. It was insultingly easy. Can you divide 144 by twelve . . . with a calculator . . . on a multiple choice test???? At first I thought they'd given me the wrong test. I had four hours to complete it, but got it done in 20 minutes. Like I said - insulting. I explained to Mr. . . . I mean BROTHER Michael that I had a "family event" later today, and couldn't make the orientation. He was ok with that. He wished me a good weekend with the most earnest smile to ever grace a human face.

I really didn't trust that guy.

My mom showed up right on time to pick me up. We got lunch and headed home. It was around this point that I was starting to get excited. It was only about six hours until I was going to see The Moody Blues!!!

After going through the nerves and anticipation of waiting for a counter-terror mission to begin, you'd think a little rock concert wouldn't be that big a deal, but I'd been wanting to see this band since I was seven years old.

As soon as my dad got home from work, I hurried him and my mom out the door. We ended up getting stuck in Dallas rush hour traffic, but I wasn't worried. We had hours to go before the show began.

The excitement started to build when I saw the first sign saying "Fair Park/Starplex Next Exit". We followed the signs, and eventually followed the line of cars into the parking lot where it seems everyone was having a tailgate party. We stopped by the T-Shirt stand, where my dad bought me a "Moody Blues MCMXC" T-Shirt with a gigantic M and B superimposed over each other. We also got pretzels and cokes - the dinner of champions. I hadn't eaten this unhealthy in months. How is it my body didn't shut down before I met Zippy?

Speaking of Zippy, we caught sight of each other about 10 seconds after my parents and I took our seats. They were one section to the right of us. I ran over and hugged her. We talked for a minute, then went to spend the rest of the evening with our respective parents. We'd compare notes on the concert later . . .

Saturday, August 25, 1990

I woke up with my ears still ringing. The concert had been great, but when it was nearly over, my dad got into a confrontation with some stoner hippie. Apparently, the hippie was mad that my dad was standing up during one of the songs, so he'd thrown a cup of ice at my dad. I didn't see this happen. I just saw my dad get up and storm out of the theater. My mom and I chased after him, but we didn't catch up till he was already to the car.

So we missed the encore.

If only I'd known about it when it happened!!!!! I'd have knocked that stoner hippie into next week!!! So why didn't my dad do anything about it? Why didn't I find out about it till we were in the car and nearly home?

I kept asking myself those questions until I remembered what Zippy said to me several months earlier in my driveway. "There are two types of people in this world. There are those who wake up in middle of night, find themselves in darkness, try to adjust their eyes, and feel their way around the room, hoping and praying they don't run into something or stub their toe. Then there are those who just turn on the damned light."

I finally understood what she meant. I also remembered her conversation with Sarah. She had been talking about me when she'd said "He was defined by his fears. He was raised by parents who are defined by THEIR fears. And he was afraid of everything."

My father couldn't have done anything other than what he did. He and my mother were exactly the same as I had been six months earlier. They ADAPTED to the darkness when it encroached. Six months ago, I was the exact same way. Somehow Zippy changed that about me.

I'd have turned around and gotten in the stoner's face if I'd realized what had happened. You don't mess with me. You definitely don't mess with my family. I'd have probably snapped the idiot's neck. I'd already killed once this summer and this guy was messing with my dad. When someone gets violent, you overwhelm them with the same. Once the line is crossed, you go all the way. When the darkness encroaches, you just turn on the light. It's the simplest and most direct solution.

Zippy and M-Gang had violently ripped me from the darkness and handed me a light-switch imprinted with the words "Never Again." I was armed with the ability to wield the powers of violence, and emboldened with an attitude that nobody is to ever hurt me or my loved ones again.

I'm not sure I could give my parents this same power. I'm not sure it would even be my place to do so if I could. But I could use it to protect people like them, people like my sister, and people like my fellow M-Gangers, from those who let darkness spread into the world through their actions.

I now understood how Zippy felt when she saw me getting beaten up four years ago. This is why I'm here. This is why I have this power. I will protect those who can't protect themselves - either from their own physical weakness, or the mental block that keeps them from turning on the lights.

I told Zippy all about this when I saw her that weekend for our regularly scheduled Sunday afternoon workout. She seemed very excited.

"You've taken the first step. You've really left the darkness behind you." She hugged me. "Congratulations."

"Don't congratulate me. You're the one who taught me this stuff."

She chuckled. "I guess so. Now is time for you to learn your first Jewish prayer."

"Huh?"

"Is first prayer that children are taught in Judaism. Is prayer you say first thing in the morning - when you come out of the darkness. Is called 'Modeh Ani.'"

EPILOGUE – A NEW DAY

Monday, August 27th, 1990, 7:00 a.m.

I'm locked in the bathroom at my parents' house. The lights are off, but the dark red heating lamp is on. The ventilator fan is running, and it's making a super loud droning hum that's threatening to lull me to sleep. I've also got the shower going so my parents think I'm . . getting a shower (which I actually did before coming home last night from training at M-Gang).

Today I'm starting a new life. I'm "born again" so to speak. I'm going to a new school, where nobody has ever heard the name "Mark Cohen." It's not D'var Adonai, but it'll do. I'll be spending Tuesday and Thursday nights at M-Gang working on my hand-to-hand combat training. Then on Wednesdays I'll be at the range - AWESOME. And at various points in between, I can be called up to go under again. I can't wait to see what the gang has in store for me this fall.

I'm nervous as hell, but they say that this thing is going to help me with my 'psych' adjustment. I've been to three different schools over the last three years, and the Mossad psych guys say that'll help me avoid the kind of attachments that get people killed in the field. But this will be my first ever experience in a "private" school. Collins Christian Academy - ick. The name alone brings up images of guys wearing polo shirts with sweaters tied around their necks on their way to tennis courts . . . with their poofy-haired gum chewing girlfriends whose eyes flash dollar signs leaning on their shoulders - yuck. Give me Tsipporah Dagan and a bunch of Israeli commandos over that any day. But I guess it beats Anderson and the death sentence that another year there would be.

The reality, of course, is that this is a bunch of weird over-religious zealots who go around calling each other "brother" this, and "brother" that. Would it be too cheesy for me to respond "oh brother?" I understand they think rock music is evil . . . as though they have an earthly idea what evil is. Yeah, in a world where PLO terrorists blow up school busses full of Israeli children, the source of all evil is . . . Def Leppard albums.

Sorry, but evil isn't found on a rock album. Evil doesn't draw pentagrams and make stupid sounding chanting noises while pretending to worship a cardboard cutout of the devil. Evil hurts. Evil whispers in the hallways. Evil giggles. Evil poisons places in your mind, and makes you think about them when you'd otherwise be happy. Evil makes you cry.

And I soundly kicked evil's ass last week!!! It's Cohen 1, Bad Guys 0.

So this is going to be an interesting ride, listening to amateurs at Collins Academy talking about how they "fight the good fight" against all the faux evil in this world that they can dream up. I actually do that, and can't tell anyone about it . . .

And that's the hard part. Other kids play video games where they pretend to do the things I actually did in real life. Other kids watch action films where overpaid actors pretend to do the stuff I really did. And I can't tell a soul. Tsipporah and I did amazing things this summer. And I can't wait to see what happens next.

I best go get dressed now. It's supposed to be a windy day. And this time of year in Dallas, that's just another thing to make it hot.

ABOUT THE AUTHOR

Do you really want to read about Robert? Mark and Zippy are much more interesting than Robert.

Okay, if you insist . . .

Robert Linus Koehl was born just outside of San Antonio, Texas, during the United States Bicentennial Celebrations. Much like Mark Cohen, he was raised in the Dallas suburb of Plano – yeah, THAT Plano. He went to college at the University of North Texas. He spent a few years working as a boring consultant. And as of this printing, he's currently pursuing a Juris Doctorate at Texas A&M University School of Law. He's also a licensed Private Investigator in the state of Texas.

Are you bored yet? STILL wanting more? Sheesh . . .

Back around 2007, he began studying Krav Maga at a school in Dallas. In 2010, the founder of a Krav Maga Children's program invited him to become an instructor. He has taught children ages six to fourteen many of the skills that Zippy taught Mark in this book.

There . . . are you happy? No? You still want more???

He still resides in Plano. Yeah . . . that Plano. Though oddly enough, his current neighborhood didn't even exist back in 1990. He excels at knowing all kinds of useless facts.

And with that, even I'm bored. Until the sequel . . .